THE MOST COVETED

THE WRITER AND BILLIONAIRE SERIES
BOOK THREE

CHARLENE ECKSTEIN

THE MOST COVETED

Charlene Eckstein

CHAPTER 1

Sascha stared out the window as she sat on another long flight across the ocean in search of Michael Ghant. Michael, her childhood friend and confidant, had betrayed her in the worst way possible. After years of false smiles, long talks, and deception, it came to light that Michael was secretly obsessed with her and had been stalking her for years. While he played the role of a sweet, supportive friend, even going as far as marrying her best friend, Cate, he had been deviously plotting ways to eliminate any romantic competitors and bring Sascha running to him.

As part of his plan, Michael partnered with Gina Campbell, a woman who secretly hated Sascha, in order to ruin Sascha's first marriage. Unfortunately for Michael, his plan backfired. Not only did Sascha not turn to him after the demise of her marriage, but instead she met Devon Montague, a handsome billionaire, and fell head over heels in love with him. As Sascha and Devon's love flourished, Michael and Gina plotted more ways to break them up, but Gina's plans for Sascha were far more sinister than

Michael's. Gina wanted Sascha dead and had made multiple attempts on her life, while Michael just wanted Sascha for himself, at any cost.

While Gina's final attempt on Sascha's life landed her in prison, Michael's part in the conspiracy remained hidden. And after Gina's suspicious death in prison, there was no one left to implicate Michael. Sascha always believed Gina had a partner but would have never guessed that person was one of her closest friends. Growing up Sascha knew Michael had feelings for her; however, she made it clear to him several times over the years that she did not return his romantic affections, which he had seemed to accept. When Sascha fixed Michael up with her best friend, Cate, she thought he was over her and loved her friend, but as it turned out, that was not the case.

Michael viewed his marriage to Cate as a means of staying close to Sascha and a way for him to bide his time until Sascha was free. Michael had waited for Sascha to love him back for over twenty years but had started to lose his patience. After Sascha and Devon married, there were two attempts on Devon's life while they honeymooned in Bali, Indonesia. And when they returned home, things got even stranger, and Sascha began to suspect Michael of not only being Gina's partner and behind the attempts on Devon's life but also trying to kill Cate. Once Michael was exposed, he made one final attempt to take Cate's life and to kidnap Sascha. Sadly for Michael both women were fighters and survived his devious attempts. Catching Michael in the act of trying to sedate Sascha to kidnap her, Devon nearly beat Michael to death, which resulted in Michael's hospitalization and arrest. Unfortunately while under arrest in the hospital, Michael managed to slip away and has been on the run ever since.

Sascha knew Michael. Regrettably. And the Michael she

knew was a determined man and would not give up, which was why she felt it was imperative that she found him before he had time to regroup and plot his revenge. There was no doubt in her mind that he was not going to let Devon have her. He would kill anyone and everyone around her before he allowed someone to stand in his way, and she had to protect them all.

Pushing dark thoughts of the past aside for a moment, Sascha looked out the plane window as they touched down. Devon and Sascha had just landed in Auckland, New Zealand, to meet with their contact. Michael had been spotted in the city days earlier but was believed to have recently left the city and traveled to Wellington, New Zealand's capital city. As Sascha listened to the discussion between Devon and the contact, she bit her lip and ran her fingers through her curly hair as her frustrations grew. They had been hunting Michael nearly nonstop for six months, and she was exhausted, both mentally and physically. Many of the leads had been dead ends, and this was likely to be another one.

Sascha wanted her life back. With the constant threat of scheming Michael, Devon barely wanted Sascha out of his sight, and he requested that she always travel with Matt, James, Tom, or Drew anywhere she went. The bodyguards were great guys, but she resented their presence at times. While Sascha and Devon drove to their hotel, with two of their four-man personal security team in tow, she closed her eyes for a few moments to calm herself before discussing their latest disappointment.

"If it really was Michael, and that's a really big if, do we have a theory on why he would be here?" Sascha asked as she looked at her husband's equally frustrated face.

"Well, we know he owns several sheep farms in Wellington, but there's no way he plans on staying there. He would easily be caught and extradited back to the United States. If it was him, there has to be something being kept on one of his properties that he needed, and he didn't trust anyone else to get it for him. But what that something could be is your best guess."

"Are we going to Wellington, then?" an exhausted Sascha asked, although she already knew the answer.

"Yes. I want to take a look around, talk to the farmhands and any other employees who might be there to verify it was him. We need to try to get an idea of why he came here."

Once they arrive at their hotel, the pair immediately freshened up, changed, and went to a private airport to fly out to Wellington. It was a one-hour flight to the capital city and then another one-hour drive by car to Michael's closest farm. The pair traveled out into the New Zealand farm country, with their personal bodyguards James and Tom following behind in a separate car. As they drove up to the first farm, Sascha saw a lot of herding activity. She noticed there were several large structures on the property, including what appeared to be a main house and another that was likely a guest house. When she stared out into the distance, Sascha could see the ocean. The farm was up against the beach.

Getting out of their rental car, Sascha and Devon headed toward a group of workers. Unfortunately, the herders were not interested. None of them would stop and talk to Sascha or Devon until finally a man, who appeared to be in charge, waved them over.

"We don't give tours at this farm," the man said as he eyed them suspiciously.

"We're not here for a tour. We're actually looking for the owner of this farm. We heard he was out here recently," Devon said to the man casually.

"Mr. Ghant? Oh, I haven't seen him in almost a year."

"So he's been to the farm in the last year? How frequently does he normally come here?" Sascha asked, hoping the man would not clam up with all their questions.

The man looked at Sascha in silence for a few moments. She worried he was about to shut down the conversation, but surprisingly he continued.

"Mr. Ghant has owned his farms here for about five years, and I have worked here the entire time. In the past five years, he has been here three times, and that includes when he first bought the farm."

"But the last time was late last year? Do you know why he came here?" Sascha pushed for more answers.

"No, I don't. Sorry I can't help you."

They thanked the man for his help and slowly walked back to their car, continuing to survey the area as they did so. Just as Sascha and Devon got back on the road to visit Michael's other two farms, Sascha heard her phone chime with an email.

"Looks like the building plans for Michael's farms have come in," Sascha said as she pulled up the email.

"Anything interesting?"

"Well, I'm no architect, but in my professional opinion, everything looks pretty standard for the two farms we're going to; however, something is up with the one we just left."

"How so?" Devon turned his handsome face to her, briefly taking his eyes off the road.

"I'm not exactly sure, but there appears to have been several revisions to the farm since Michael purchased it. And I mean a lot of demolition and construction has gone on there, but I can't tell what is different besides the additional structure on the far end of the property."

Devon pulled the car over, and Sascha handed him her phone. He studied the images in silence for several minutes. She studied him and could not resist running her fingers through his dark, wavy hair. He glanced up briefly and smiled at her before returning his focus to the phone. He zoomed in and out of the images multiple times before handing her back her phone. Devon started the car again, signaled to the bodyguards, and immediately made a U-turn.

"Where are we going?"

"We're going to that beach behind the farm," Devon responded with a focused expression on his face.

"Why?"

"Because I think there are tunnels running from that new structure down to the beach. If my guess is right, there is a cave on that beach that will lead us to a house on the farm."

The pair drove to a cliff area on the backside of Michael's property. As Devon explained to James and Drew what they were about to do, with instructions to come looking for them if they did not physically see them for twenty minutes, Sascha found a somewhat safe spot to traverse down the twenty feet to the sandy earth. It was challenging getting down to the beach for the pair as they encountered steep terrain, having to climb down and over sharp rocks. Once they landed on the beach, the wind whipped Sasha's brown hair around her face as the cooler air numbed her skin. The sunshine made the golden high-lights in her hair shimmer but did little to warm her body. She zipped up her jacket and put her hands in her pockets for warmth while staring down the beach, observing several cave openings.

Walking down the coastline to the first cave opening, Sascha began to get nervous.

"Is this wise?" she asked her husband.

"Probably not," Devon replied as he chuckled. "You ready?"

"Yes, but let me send Brina a quick text message letting her know what we're doing…just in case."

"Good idea. I'll let James know we're going into a tunnel and where they can recover our bodies," he said as he texted.

"Not funny," Sascha responded as they both turned on their phone flashlights in preparation for the darkness of the caves. The couple stood and stared into the cave entrance, listening for any noises coming out of it, but they were met with silence. Phone in one hand and a small can of pepper spray in the other, Sascha took a deep breath and followed her husband into the darkness.

The cave was pitch-black and damp, and it had a familiar smell about it. The cave smelled wonderfully earthy and fresh. Shining their lights from their phones, Sascha and Devon scanned the cave. The cave was actually quite lovely, with moss-covered rocks and the sound of trickling water. The humidity in the cave warmed Sascha slightly, and she shined her light to the top of the cave, hoping to not find bats. Not finding any immediate threats, the couple moved deeper into the cavernous space until they came to a fork in the cave.

"Well, which way now?" Devon said as he stopped and looked to his wife.

Sascha shined her flashlight down each path. The path to the right seemed to move away from the Ghant farm, but the left one appeared to lead directly to it.

"This way." She pointed and started down the cave before waiting for a response from her husband.

After walking for about a minute, Devon stopped Sascha.

"I think this cave has been traveled recently," he said as he shined his light up the cave walls and spotted mounted torch holders and torches.

They stood in place and examined the area. The walls were damp, but someone had taken the time to wrap the torches in a protective plastic to keep them from getting wet. Just as Sascha was about to turn her focus forward again, she noticed a small, dark object on the floor. Shining her light directly on it, it appeared to be a cloth of some sort.

"What is that?" Devon asked as Sascha bent to pick the object up.

"Well, it looks like…a mask, I think," Sascha responded as she observed the demimask, which is often found at masquerade balls. She turned the mask over in her hand and found the front of it to be gold, sparkly, and very pretty.

"Hmm, well, the plot thickens," Devon said as he started walking again.

It was not long before the pair came upon gates in front of a door that clearly led into a house on Michael's property. They shook the gates and searched for a possible hidden key close by, but their efforts were futile. Deciding to return to the beach, Sascha and Devon quickly departed the cave.

Exiting the cave, it was noticeably colder and darker than it had been before they entered it.

"It's going to be dark soon. We should get back to the city."

Sascha nodded her head and followed her husband back up the steep rocks. Fortunately they were both athletic and in excellent shape, which allowed them to make quick work of the climb. As they walked back to the car, Sascha pulled the mask out of her pocket and rubbed the soft, velvety material between her fingers. The faint scent of an expensive perfume still lingered.

"A wealthy woman wore this mask," Sascha stated as she looked to Devon.

"What was a well-to-do woman doing in that cave?" Devon asked with a puzzled expression on this face.

"Up to no good is my guess," Sascha said as she chuckled, and they got into the car.

CHAPTER 2

$\mathcal{I}$t had been two weeks since Sascha and Devon returned from their trip to New Zealand, and although they were finally getting back into their regular routine, Sascha had to admit the search for Michael was taking its toll on them as a couple. While the tunnels found on Michael's New Zealand property could possibly be a lead to something, for the moment, the trip appeared to be another dead end. Neither of them wanted to stop searching for their friend turned enemy who tried to destroy their lives, but Sascha had a feeling she was giving Michael just what he had always wanted. He was at the center of her life and always on her mind.

As Sascha sat, thinking about all that had transpired over the last six months, she held the mask she found in the cave in her hand. The mask was a clue, but to what she had no idea. She had Tatum searching for a retailer of the mask and had finally identified the perfume, and it was just as she had thought. The perfume was a very expensive and exclusive fragrance.

Devon was not particularly interested in finding the

mask's owner and had said as much. He was singularly focused on finding Michael, and so was Sascha, but she believed the cave, the mask, and Michael's ability to evade the law were all intertwined. To Sascha's chagrin, they could not see eye to eye on this topic and decided to agree to disagree.

Devon was back to being a busy businessman during the day, while Sascha worked on her fifth book in her Coven of Plumvale series. During her lunchtime, Sascha spent time with her nearly three-year-old daughter, Danielle, who was in the early stages of preschool and would soon start attending an elite school known for having students with high-profile parents as well as for maintaining heavy security at their campus. The thought of her little girl growing up both scared and excited Sascha, and with Michael still on the loose, Sascha was never comfortable having Danielle out of her sight. With Michael's state of mind, she would not put it past him to take her little girl to use as leverage to get Sascha into his clutches. And it would work too because there was nothing Sascha would not do for Devon and Danielle.

Sitting in her home office writing, with her two cats Toffee and Greer at her feet, Sascha heard a quick knock before the door opened. Devon walked in with a distressed look on his face.

"What's wrong?" Sascha asked as she stood up and went over to him.

"Emma has been admitted to the hospital, and it doesn't look good," Devon stated as he dropped his head, and Sascha pulled him into a hug.

Emma Harper had been Devon's personal assistant for nearly ten years and was like a mother figure to him and a family member for both Devon and Sascha. She was an older woman and had adult children near Sascha's and Devon's ages, but she had refused to retire. She did, however, recently agree to cut back on her hours and traveling with Devon on business trips in the past year as her health had been declining.

"We should pack and go to London now before it's too late," Sascha told Devon as he squeezed her tighter in the hug.

Within two hours, Devon, Sascha, Danielle, their bodyguards Matt and Tom, and their nanny Lena were on a private jet to London, England. Ten hours later, the group arrived at a foggy and rainy London. The somber weather fit the group's mood. Devon reached out to Emma's oldest son immediately upon landing and was told to come straight to the hospital as the doctors did not expect his mother to last much longer. Sascha took Danielle, Lena, Tom, and Matt to their London townhouse while Devon went on to the hospital. She planned to meet Devon at the hospital once she got Danielle settled in but worried she would not make it in time to say goodbye before Emma's passing.

An hour later, sitting in the back of a town car on her way to the hospital, Sascha received a text from Devon informing her Emma had died. While Sascha silently cried in the back of the car, she frantically searched her purse for tissues, and Matt reached back from the front seat and handed her what she sought. Sascha thanked Matt as tears continued to stream heavily from her eyes. Matt was always very kind to Sascha. She reminded herself to thank and appreciate all the wonderful people in her life more frequently before they, too, were gone.

Finally arriving at the hospital, Sascha rushed into Devon's arms, and they held one another tightly. As Sascha and Devon comforted one another, there was no need for words between them. After holding on to her for a few more moments, Devon took her by the hand and led her to a set of chairs. Sascha did not see Emma's children when she arrived, but she did not want to leave before offering her support and condolences. The couple patiently sat in a waiting area as they wanted to give Emma's children their privacy to grieve. After about an hour of Emma's children speaking with doctors, filling out paperwork, and making arrangements, they came out to talk with the Montagues.

Sascha immediately offered her condolences and hugs to Emma's children Christopher, Amelia, and Henry. After everyone gathered themselves, Amelia stated she was still in shock because just the other day her mother seemed to be getting better, and then out of nowhere, she took a sudden turn for the worse. Shaking her head in disbelief, Amelia motioned to her older brother to speak. Christopher tried to speak, but he became too choked up to do so, which prompted his sister, Amelia, to take over the discussion. Amelia informed Sascha and Devon that their mother had already made all her own funeral arrangements and stated that she hoped they would stay in the country for the funeral, which was to be held at the end of the week. The Montagues had always intended to stay and say their farewells to Emma and offered any needed support to her children, financial or otherwise.

The Montagues said their goodbyes and turned to depart when Christopher stopped them. "Oh, I almost forgot," he said as he handed Devon two white envelopes. "These were with my mother's things, and both are addressed to you."

Devon glanced down at the envelopes in hand but did not say a word. He just nodded and once again bid Emma's children farewell.

Departing the hospital, Sascha and Devon sat silently in the back of their car as their driver drove them back to the townhouse. The Montagues arrived back at their London home after midnight. The house was quiet as they made their way up to their daughter's room. Checking in on her, they found Danielle fast asleep and Lena sleeping in a chair with one of Sascha's books on her lap in the corner of the room. While Devon went to give his daughter kisses, Sascha gently woke Lena up, thanked her, and sent her off to her room. It had been a long day for all of them.

Arriving to their room, Sascha closed the door behind them as she watched her husband sit on the edge of the bed and put his face into his hands. She knew he was devastated by the loss of Emma but also realized he was not yet ready to talk about it. Devon had suffered much loss throughout his life. He was an only child whose father abandoned him and his mother when he was young. It had been just Devon and his mother for most of his life as she never remarried. Sadly Devon's mother passed away while he was in college, and his mother's sister was his only remaining family on his mother's side, and he had no relationship with anyone on his father's side.

Sascha sat down next to her husband and put her arm around him. They sat quietly for a few moments before Devon stood up and said he needed a shower. He bent down to kiss Sascha before heading into the bathroom. Sascha started to gather her toiletries as she heard the glass shower door open. Deciding to join her husband, she quickly undressed and followed him out of the bedroom.

Walking into the bathroom, Sascha could barely see her husband in the shower as the glass was all steamed up. Opening the shower door, she stepped into the large enclosure while her husband stood under the rain shower with his eyes closed as he allowed the hot water to cascade over his body. Sascha poured shower gel into her hands, created a lather, and began running her hands up and down Devon's back, adding pressure to her touch and lightly massaging his tense muscles. Wanting to comfort Devon, Sascha pressed her body against his and laid her cheek against his wet back while wrapping her arms around his waist. He relaxed in her embrace before suddenly turning around with fire in his eyes. Devon pulled Sascha into his arms as his lips passionately kissed her full mouth. Sascha melted into his embrace while he pressed her body against the cold marble shower wall. Devon lifted her up, and Sascha wrapped her long legs around his waist as her eager body prepared for penetration. Sascha cried out in pleasure as Devon entered her, and she held on tightly as the vigorous lovemaking commenced. Stress, grief, fear, and desire all met to create a powerful physical union they both needed. As water continued to pour over their bodies, they held each other's gaze as they found their release. Moans turned to soft kisses and loving words as they descended back down to earth together. After their passion subsided, they washed each other's body in silence.

Once out of the shower and dressed for bed, Devon shared how devastated he felt about the loss of Emma but said she would not want him to be spending too much time grieving. Emma was always pragmatic. Sascha and Devon agreed they would be sad and grieve for the week, but after the funeral, they planned to find ways to celebrate and honor Emma's life.

The following morning, Sascha woke up early, while Devon continued to sleep. Glancing at the nightstand, she noticed the two letters from Emma still remained unread. Sascha's heart broke for her husband. After changing into her workout clothes, Sascha went downstairs to their small home gym, which contained a treadmill, an exercise bike, and two racks of free weights. Sascha's exercise of choice was always running, although she did mix it up sometimes. After spending ten minutes stretching, she hopped onto the treadmill, put in her earbuds, and began her five-mile run.

While Sascha ran, she tried to clear her mind, but recent events held her thoughts captive. Michael Ghant and his continued threat was always a distraction. No matter how hard she tried not to think about him, there he was, in some corner of her mind. The only way she would ever feel safe again would be if Michael was behind bars or dead. At this point she did not care which one. They had to find him at all costs. And there was no doubt in her mind that there would be a high price to pay.

CHAPTER 3

By the time Sascha came out of the gym, she could smell breakfast cooking. As she walked closer, she heard her adorable daughter's voice and smelled brewing coffee. Sascha walked into the breakfast room to find Devon and Danielle sitting at the table eating. As Danielle ate a waffle, Devon sipped his coffee while he read one of the two letters from Emma.

Sascha went into the room and said good morning and smooched both of her daughter's cheeks as her daughter giggled that Mommy was sweaty. Devon glanced up and said good morning too but appeared to be deep in thought. Sascha gave him a gentle kiss before saying she needed to go take a quick shower. Devon said okay but kept staring at the letter in his hand.

Sascha went upstairs to her room, curious about the letters' contents, but she wanted to give Devon time to digest whatever they contained before asking him questions about them. Sascha did not have to wait long to find out what the letters said as she found Devon sitting on the small sofa in their room after she exited the bathroom. Wrapped in a soft terry-cloth robe, she sat beside him ready to listen.

"As you are aware," he started, "Emma left me two letters. In the first letter, she said how I was like a son to her and that she considered me family, which was why she had refused to retire. She goes on to say how wonderful you and Danielle are and how much she loved you both. She then discusses a few personal items she wants us to have and asked that I continue to stay in touch with her children and for me to look out for them."

Devon paused for a long while, which made Sascha prod him to continue. "And the second letter?"

"Apparently she has already selected her replacement to be my personal assistant. Some woman named Delilah Cahill," he said with a look of disbelief.

"Well, are you surprised? Emma was like a general. She was always prepared and had a plan for everything. Why would her death be any different?" Sascha asked.

"No, you're right. She was always on task, often early in fact, but I guess I am a bit surprised that she has never mentioned this person to me before."

"It is a little surprising, and I can understand your reluctance to take on someone new so soon, and no one will ever replace Emma, but if this is who she is recommending, the woman is probably a solid choice. She's here in London, and we're here in London, so I suggest we meet this Delilah Cahill and give her a chance as was Emma's wish. Besides, if she turns out not to be a good fit, you can let her go. Emma would understand that too."

Despite Devon's hesitancy to consider taking on Delilah Cahill, he called her to set up a meeting with her, him, and Sascha. The person selected to be Devon's personal assistant would spend a lot of time traveling with him and would be around the Montague household and their family frequently. Sascha loved and appreciated that it was important to Devon that she gave her stamp of approval on whoever that person was to be but was surprised by his hesitation. He had been needing a new assistant since Emma became ill, and Emma herself had handpicked Delilah Cahill. Deciding to let the matter drop, Sascha figured it was best to just meet the woman and go from there.

Delilah Cahill arrived at the Montagues' residence fifteen minutes early for her appointment at 3:00 p.m. The housekeeper let her in and showed her to Devon's home office, where she would wait for him and Sascha to join her. Sascha was getting Danielle up from her nap and was unable to join Devon and Ms. Cahill right away. After getting Danielle her afternoon snack, Sascha handed Danielle over to Lena and went to meet with Devon and Ms. Cahill in his office. Sascha walked at a quick pace to her destination but slowed as she approached the door to Devon's office when she heard him laughing, which was an unexpected sound.

As Sascha entered the room, both Devon and Ms. Cahill stood up to greet her. Devon introduced Sascha to Delilah Cahill as his wonderful wife and partner. Sascha blushed as she turned to meet Ms. Cahill and was caught completely off guard by her appearance. Delilah Cahill was younger than expected and a stunning beauty. Delilah Cahill had long, dark hair pulled back into a tight, full bun. She wore large black-rimmed glasses, a dark pantsuit, and diamond stud earrings.

Despite the intentional, or possibly unintentional, camouflage she used to distract from her beauty, it was obvious she was a gorgeous woman. She wore makeup that looked professionally applied and had big blue eyes that stood out on her small oval face. Delilah Cahill was an inch shorter than Sascha's five-foot-nine height, was thin, and had large, perfectly round breasts. Yes, Delilah Cahill was definitely not what Sascha had been expecting.

Sascha sat down in a chair next to Delilah Cahill, and they began to discuss how she knew Emma. Delilah Cahill stated she knew Emma from their previous employer, a large London-based financial firm where Emma had been her mentor. As Sascha listened to Delilah Cahill speak about her educational background at elite schools and her excellent references, Sascha could not help but feel suspicious of her. She seemed too good to be true in Sascha's opinion, but she pushed those feelings aside as this was a person Emma had recommended, and Sascha had nothing but respect for Emma and her judgment. Ultimately it would be Devon's decision, and deep down Sascha was hoping he would decide not to hire this woman.

"Ms. Cahill, why do you want to take this job with Devon and leave your home here, when there are plenty of other opportunities for you in the United Kingdom and in Europe?"

Delilah Cahill nodded her head and smiled sweetly before answering. "As you are aware, I have a master's degree in business administration with an emphasis in finance and accounting, and I have entrepreneurial goals. Mr. Montague is one of the most successful businessmen in the world, and I know I could learn so much just from working with him. This really is an opportunity of a lifetime," she said as she flashed a perfect smile. "Oh, and please call me Delilah."

Sascha nodded her head and smiled in return. She kind of hated her. *Am I just jealous and feeling threatened?* she thought to herself. She trusted Devon completely, unlike her ex-husband, Lucas Gills, but she was not so sure that Ms. Cahill was trustworthy. In fact, she seemed fake and reminded Sascha of her dead nemesis, Gina Campbell.

After interviewing Delilah Cahill for nearly an hour, Sascha and Devon showed her out and promised to be in touch. The moment the door closed behind the woman, Sascha turned to face Devon and said, "So?"

"I think she's great. I mean, she's no Emma, but she could come close with time. What did you think of her?"

"She was more than qualified and quite beautiful, but if I am being completely honest, I'm not sure about her."

"I didn't notice her looks," Devon started as Sascha raised her eyebrows and made a face that said she was not buying what he was saying.

"Okay, yes, I could see she was attractive, but my thought on that is that it's not a big deal. I am married to the sexiest, most beautiful woman in the world who men would kill to have, literally. What do I care about another pretty face? But if you don't like her or it bothers you, we don't need to hire her. There are plenty of other candidates to choose from," Devon stated as he pulled Sascha into his arms.

While Sascha did not want him to hire Delilah, she also did not want to seem jealous and petty or penalize another woman just because she happened to be pretty. So despite her gut feelings, she told Devon that she agreed Delilah was a great candidate and that she supported hiring her.

"Are you sure? I do not want to ever make you feel uncomfortable with a situation or create any trust issues between us in the future. I know what Lucas did to you, and I don't want you to ever think that I could be that guy."

"I know you're nothing like him, and that never crossed my mind," Sascha responded slowly as she thought for another moment. "I say let's give Delilah a chance and see how it works out. She may turn out to be a great fit."

"Consider it done," Devon said, and he pulled Sascha into a sensual kiss. "I love you so much," he whispered in her ear as he pressed her body against the front door.

Sascha returned her frisky husband's passionate kiss, but in the back of her mind, she feared she had just made a terrible mistake.

CHAPTER 4

$\mathcal{A}$fter returning from London, Sascha knew she needed a session with a therapist. Her current therapist was Dr. James Benedict. Dr. Benedict specialized in treating survivors of traumatic events, and between her harassment and being shot by Gina Campbell and Michael Ghant's assault and attempt to kidnap her, Sascha had a lot of trauma to process. While Dr. Benedict's session had helped her in the past, since learning Dr. Benedict may have started dating Sascha's friend and neighbor Anna Green, Sascha now felt leery of him and his motivations.

Sascha called Dr. Benedict's office and made an appointment with him for later in the week, but today she was having Anna over for brunch in her garden, and then they were going for a long, therapeutic walk in their neighborhood. Sascha was fortunate to live in an exclusive, gated community known as the Swell. It was a coveted yet magical place to live, and Sascha had yet to explore all the Swell had to offer.

When Anna joined Sascha that morning for brunch, she was in good spirits. Anna had just finalized her divorce from her husband, Tomas, a world-renowned neurosurgeon and medical device inventor, and had been awarded full custody of their twin daughters as well as ownership of their luxurious home, which sat across the street from Sascha's. Sascha suspected that some of Anna's joy was due to the man she was secretly dating, and while Anna had declined to confirm Sascha's suspicions of the man's identity in the past, Sascha was almost certain the secret lover was none other than Sascha's therapist, Dr. James Benedict.

If Sascha's hunch turned out to be right, Dr. Benedict would have a lot of questions to answer. Based on the timeline of the relationship, Dr. Benedict started pursuing a relationship with Anna right after he started seeing Sascha as a patient. And it was no secret that Anna had also been a victim of Gina Campbell. Anna had been Gina's therapist and was used as bait to lure an unsuspecting Sascha away from her home and away from her bodyguard. Whatever the reason was for this new Anna, Sascha had to admit that she looked amazing and told her so.

Anna blushed and said thank you as she gave Sascha a tight hug and then handed her a bottle of Sascha's favorite prosecco. As the women headed to the kitchen area to make their plates, Devon popped in to say good morning to Anna and to snag a croissant from a platter. Before leaving, he planted a kiss on Sascha's lips and then went back to his office.

"Wow, I'm so jealous. You two are such a hot couple," Anna stated as she watched Devon walk away.

"Well, keep in mind we are technically still in our honeymoon phase," Sascha responded as she chuckled and began to make mimosas with the prosecco Anna brought, adding fresh-squeezed orange juice to their glasses.

The look on Anna's face told Sascha she did not believe her words.

"And our relationship has been full of nonstop drama thanks to Gina and Michael," Sascha stated as she handed Anna her drink and took a sip of her own.

"Tomas and I were never like that. No, trust me, what you two have is different…it's special. I truly envy that, but I am so happy for you."

Sascha smiled as she pondered Anna's words and thought her friend had just given her the perfect opening to ask questions about her secret beau.

"Speaking of relationships, how are you and your mystery man doing?"

A pained look crossed Anna's face, making Sascha regret her question. Deciding to quickly change the subject, Sascha instructed Anna to grab her plate so they could go sit outside in the garden and enjoy their brunch and the views out in the morning sun. Once the ladies were seated, Sascha glanced out over the cliffs in the distance of her backyard and admired the ocean views. The ocean called to her, and she never tired of the feeling it gave her. Breathing in the salty air, Sascha felt instantly calm and at ease.

"We're not seeing each other anymore," Anna said as she stared out into the distance as well.

"Oh, I'm sorry. I shouldn't have pried. I did not mean to upset you."

"That's the thing; I'm not upset. I guess I'm just really disappointed."

"I thought you were crazy about him," Sascha said, finding it hard to believe Anna was not more upset over the breakup.

"I was…for a time. But then I realized we were not compatible, and there was something else," Anna said with a curious expression on her face.

Anna's statement intrigued Sascha, and she needed to know more. "Something else? What do you mean?"

"I know this sounds crazy, but I started to feel like I was part of some sort of an agenda or school project for him. He was charming and romantic, and he always said the right things, but it felt false. Rehearsed. He knew I had a huge crush on him all those years ago when we worked on our doctorate. He knew I also had suffered trauma, and he knew I was vulnerable. I mean, who's better at manipulation and mind games than a psychiatrist? But of course I recognized what was happening once I came out of the fog."

"Can I ask you something?"

"Of course," Anna quickly responded.

"Was it Dr. James Benedict you were seeing?"

A shocked expression crossed Anna's face. "How did you know?"

Without answering Anna's questions, Sascha continued. "Did he tell you he was my therapist?"

"What? No!"

Anna sat quietly for a few moments before she let out a laugh.

"What's so funny?" Sascha asked, completely confused by Anna's sudden laughter.

"This is a relief. I thought my instincts were failing me, but I was right about him all along. He had an agenda."

Sascha scrunched her face at Anna's statement. "And what agenda was that?"

"You, Sascha. You were his agenda. You know he never asked about you directly, but he did ask lots of questions about the night with Gina, which of course led me to talk about you. Quite devious of him now that I think about it, but he must have been smitten with you. And probably still is I am guessing."

"Anna, I'm really sorry he did this to you. I know how much you liked him," Sascha said as she placed her hand on Anna's. "And smitten or not, his behavior has been completely unethical and stalkerish too. He is no better than Michael," Sascha stated in disgust.

"Don't be sorry. You did nothing wrong. I was more in love with the idea of him from over twenty years ago than I was with the man he is today. In reality we had nothing in common besides being psychiatrists. I found him quite boring. And you're right; he is no better than Michael Ghant," Anna responded as she shook her head. "We can report him to the state board. Is that something you think you would want to do?" Anna said gently.

"No," Sascha responded, unsure how she wanted to handle the situation. She had not even told Devon about her suspicions of Dr. Benedict. "Well, at least not before I confront him. I'm so confused about why he would do all of this."

"Well, in case you have not figured it out, you, my dear, are the girl most coveted," Anna said as a matter of fact.

"I'm not sure what you mean by that, but it sounds ridiculous," Sascha said, feeling oddly self-conscious.

"Some women just have this strange hold over men, and you are one of those women. Men cannot resist you. They will do anything to have you. And to tell you the truth, I used to envy women like you with your beauty and charm and intelligence. It always seemed so unfair. You got it all, but nothing comes without a cost, I suppose."

"Ugh, well I don't want to be coveted. I don't want any other man than the one I have. I just want to live happily ever after with Devon."

"And I believe you will have that, my friend, some day. Just not yet."

"Okay, this conversation is getting depressing. How about we go for that walk now?" Sascha said as she stood up and gulped down the rest of her mimosa.

It was a perfect day for a walk through the Swell, which

sat on priceless acres of breathtaking land with a small forest full of trails on one side of the property and cliffs and oceans views on the other side. Looking out into the San Francisco Bay, Sascha could not help but smile as they started off on their walk. Being in the Swell was like being cocooned in a blanket of beauty and luxury, completely cut off from the rest of the world and all the unpleasantness that existed in it.

The morning fog had started to clear, and the sun was shining through, but there was still a coolness in the air that kept the body from overheating while walking briskly. While Sascha and Anna walked and talked about their kids and work, they saw familiar faces coming their way. It was the Bougie Mafia approaching. Usually just three women, Sascha noticed an additional woman named Gillian Crafts was with the clique this morning. Sascha had met the newcomer a few times out and about in society, but Gillian Crafts did not live in the Swell. The woman stood out to Sascha because she always fangirled over Sascha every time they met, making her a little uncomfortable. And walking with Bougie Mafia beauties, she stood out even more.

The Bougie Mafia consisted of three women who lived in the Swell. Lucy Bates, Marissa Tanner, and Kerri Carter were young and attractive and lived to flash their wealth. The women power walked through the neighborhood as a group on a daily basis and were sure to chat up any neighbor they passed on the way.

Lucy Bates was married to a wealthy tech giant, and she never failed to mention that she was also an actress, although Sascha had not seen her in anything new in years. She was blond with a pixie cut, had fair skin with freckles, and had a slim model's figure on a very tall frame. Lucy had a warm aura about her, which was why Sascha was surprised she could stand hanging around with the other two.

Marissa Tanner was married to a much older man who

spent much of his time at their home in Florida. Marissa was a former beauty queen, whose current claim to fame was as a social media influencer. She posted daily about her wonderful life in the Swell, which Sascha was pretty sure was against the Swell's bylaws, and frequently showcased her expensive home, clothing, and décor. With her long, thick mahogany hair, surgically enhanced figure, and beautiful face, Marissa could have just about any man she wanted, and unfortunately for many women, the men she wanted tended to be someone else's husband. Marissa was the high school mean girl parading around as a respectable socialite.

Kerri Carter was the one in the clique Sascha found the most out of place. Kerri was a Harvard-educated lawyer who was married to a wealthy senator. Although she had given up her career as a federal prosecutor to be a stay-at-home mom and to support her wealthy husband's political ambitions, she spent most of her days with two women she seemed to have nothing in common with. Kerri was petite, with straight brown hair and a big pretty smile, but Sascha sensed she was the real firecracker of the group. Not someone to be trifled with.

Once the women came upon each other, they stopped for small talk. Lucy was the most friendly and talkative, while Marissa plastered a fake smile on her face and told Sascha and Anna how great they looked, then recommended they check out some of her beauty tutorials online. The back-handed compliments did not go unnoticed. Sascha just blankly stared at Marissa and thought, *What a bitch!* As the group all stood there, Sascha smelled a familiar scent. One of the women was wearing the perfume she had smelled on the mask found in the New Zealand tunnel. As she tried to scooch closer to the women to figure out who was wearing the scent, she got distracted.

Gillian gave both Anna and Sascha hugs and seemed

genuinely happy to see them. Gillian had inky black hair with blunt-cut bangs, she wore black-rimmed glasses that magnified her dark eyes, and she had a thick body on a short frame. Given Gillian's average appearance and lack of the Swell residency, Sascha was surprised the Bougie Mafia would hang out with her. As Sascha pondered the odd friendship and mysterious perfume lingering in the air, Gillian rambled on about how she could not wait for Sascha's next book and new series to premiere and how she wished she lived in the Swell so they could hang out more.

Kerri was noticeably quiet during the meetup and seemed detached from the group. Sascha tried to engage her in conversation, but she appeared to have something else on her mind and told the entire group she was not feeling well and promptly left in the opposite direction. Lucy and Marissa flashed curious looks at one another, said their goodbyes, and continued on with their walk, with Gillian reluctantly following behind them.

Once Sascha and Anna were alone again, Sascha asked, "How can you stand being in Marissa's presence after her affair with Tomas?"

"I can't stand her, but she was one of many for Tomas. She is trash, but she will get what's coming to her someday. That I know for sure," sweet Anna said without emotion.

Anna's words sent chills down Sascha's spine. Gone was the passive Anna who Sascha had met three years ago, and in her place was a fierce and perhaps vengeful woman, whom Sascha liked even more.

"What do you think about that Gillian woman hanging out with them?"

"I think it's weird and suspect."

"Hmm, weird and suspect indeed," Sascha said, laughing as they kept walking.

After walking four miles, the women ended up back at Sascha's home just as Delilah Cahill was arriving.

"Who's that?" Anna asked as she observed the beauty.

"Oh, that's Delilah Cahill, Devon's new personal assistant," Sascha said as she watched through squinted eyes while the beautiful woman exited her car.

"Umm, okay. Well, girl, all I can say is you are braver than me," Anna stated with a wide-eyed expression as she gave Sascha a quick hug before walking across the street to her house, leaving Sascha standing in her driveway with a pit in the bottom of her stomach.

CHAPTER 5

Sascha loved to exercise and used fitness as a stress reliever. In the past year, Sascha had kicked it up a notch by adding Krav Maga training to her workout regime. Krav Maga is an Israeli martial art, derived from combing multiple martial art disciplines, and it is meant to finish a fight as quickly and as aggressively as possible. Sascha was initially trained in Krav Maga by a world-renowned expert and was now fully capable of disarming an attacker and killing a man with her bare hands, although she hoped to never have to do it. As Sascha progressed in levels and her skill set, the training difficulty increased, and she was now starting weapons training. Although Sascha did not care for guns, she still trained with firearms and knew how to use them effectively. But her real weapon of choice was a knife. She loved learning to fight with knives. Matt, her bodyguard, had trained in Krav Maga during his time serving in the military special forces, and when Sascha's trainer was not around, he served as her sparring partner.

On this day Sascha and Matt were working on disarming an attacker with a knife to your throat, and then using that knife to incapacitate the assailant. Matt was bigger, stronger, and slightly taller than Sascha, but she held her own because she was faster and a quick thinker. After Sascha managed to stun Matt with a headbutt and drop down to a knee to twist his wrist back hard enough to force him to release the knife, Matt put his free hand up in concession.

"You're getting really good at this," Matt said as he rubbed his face while blood trickled down to his lip.

"Thank you. Now let me get you an ice pack for that nose," Sascha stated with a grimace as she ran off to the kitchen.

SASCHA HAD BEEN AVOIDING Dr. Benedict since their last session. Although sessions with him had helped her find ways to cope with anger and trauma and to move on from the Gina Campbell situation, she knew she could not see him anymore. There were too many red flags about Dr. Benedict and his behavior, and she could not trust him anymore. Not only had he started dating her friend and neighbor Anna under false pretenses, but Sascha believed he had been attempting to manipulate her throughout their sessions.

Dr. Benedict had messaged her multiple times over the past few months, expressing concern as he had seen the news about Michael. Sascha appreciated his concern, but in one of his many messages, he stated that he missed her. Sascha was no psychiatrist, but she was fairly certain that Dr. Benedict was crossing some professional boundaries, and while she did not plan to continue seeing him after today's session, she needed answers from him before she could move on.

Sascha walked into Dr. Benedict's office and was once again struck by how attractive he was. Dr. Benedict was fifty years old with a tall, lean, and extremely fit body for a man his age. He had salt-and-pepper hair, a low-cut beard, and soft gray eyes that invited trust. But as it turned out, Dr. Benedict was anything but trustworthy.

After her last session with Dr. Benedict, Sascha had a private investigator look into him, and it came to light that he had lied to her about several things from his past. He did not have a fiancée who died like he had heartbreakingly confessed to her, but he had been married and divorced twice. And one of his ex-wives was a former patient.

Based on the private investigator's report, Dr. Benedict had a habit of having romantic relationships with his patients. He was a predator. He treated patients, mostly women, who were trauma victims and emotionally vulnerable. He preyed on those women. He lured them in, seduced them, and then dropped them when he lost interest, leaving them worse off than how he found them.

"Sascha, it's so good to see you," Dr. Benedict said cheerfully. "Please have a seat."

Sascha sat down in her usual spot and kept a neutral face. She did not intend to confront the doctor right away. Her phone was recording the conversation, and she wanted to give him as much opportunity as possible to expose his true self. They sat in silence for nearly a minute staring at one another. While Sascha scrutinized the doctor, Dr. Benedict admired Sascha's beauty and appeared to be giddy with joy to be in her presence once again. Not sure if the stare down was a power play, but Sascha refused to break eye contact, forcing Dr. Benedict to do so first as he stammered out his first words of their session.

"I know you have been through a lot since we have last spoken, and I want you to know that I am here for you. I have thought about you every day since our last session. I had hoped you would call me, but I realize you were likely still processing the recent events and this new trauma."

She meekly nodded her head while Dr. Benedict continued to talk.

"I'm going to ask you a series of questions, and I know they may seem very personal, but I have to ask them so that I may offer the best treatment plan for you."

"Of course. What are your questions?"

"Did Mr. Ghant physically assault you?"

"Yes, I suppose," Sascha slowly responded, and her thoughts flashed back to that night. "He did not hit me or anything like that, but he did inject me with ketamine to drug me. To take me."

Dr. Benedict showed no reaction to her answer but continued to stare at her intensely.

"Did Mr. Ghant sexually assault you?"

"He tried," Sascha answered, and her pulse started racing. She did not like thinking about the night Michael attacked her, and she did not like where this line of questioning was heading.

"And has this affected your intimacy with your husband?"

"I'm not sure I know what you mean," Sascha responded, even though she knew exactly what he meant.

"Are you and your husband still having sex?"

She knew what he was hoping she would say and decided to play along. "No, we have not been intimate since before Michael's attack."

Although he kept his facial expression neutral, Dr. Benedict's eyes glowed with joy and excitement at her words.

"Well, intimacy is very important for couples," Dr. Benedict said, and then he paused briefly as if he was choosing his next words carefully. "If you are open to it, I have some techniques that I think you might find helpful."

"Helpful for?" Sascha asked.

"Getting your and your husband's sex life back on track."

"Really? Such as?" Sascha could almost guess where this

was going, and she wanted to scream her head off at the audacity of the man.

"Hypnotherapy is one option. I could put you under hypnosis and help alleviate some of your intimacy fears on your subconscious level."

"And how would you do that? By suggestion?"

"Well, yes. Suggestion is a very powerful tool. And we would discuss beforehand what suggestions I would implant," Dr. Benedict replied as he eyed Sascha like an animal eyeing its prey.

"If suggestions under hypnosis are as powerful as you say they are, how could I protect myself from suggestions being implanted that I do not desire?"

"That's a very good question," Dr. Benedict responded, and Sascha could tell he was thrown off by her question. He tried to stall to come up with a good response before he continued. "Sascha, the relationship between a patient and their therapist is one of total trust. I will always have your best interest at heart and would never betray you as some others have."

Bullshit, Sascha thought.

"Okay, and the other choice?" Sascha responded coolly. There was no way in hell she would trust this man to put her under hypnosis.

Dr. Benedict leaned forward in his chair and spoke softly. "I can act as a surrogate for your husband and help you work through your trauma physically with me." Dr. Benedict's words sounded so clinical and sincere that Sascha could almost believe them. Almost.

"So you mean you would have sex with me?" Sascha asked, wanting the clarification for her recording.

"Well, it would be whatever you desire. Whatever you would do to your husband, or have him do to you, you would use me in his stead, and I would coach you through it. It's all for therapeutic purposes of course. You can trust me."

"You keep using the word trust, and I just don't trust you." Sascha finally let some of her anger show.

"Sascha, I derive no pleasure from being a surrogate. It would all be for you," Dr. Benedict responded in an even, gentle tone.

"Really? Is that why I see an erection in your pants?" Sascha said as she started laughing hysterically, which made Dr. Benedict sit back in his seat.

He placed his notepad over his lap as his face turned red.

"Did you know Gina Campbell?"

"What? Of course not," Dr. Benedict stated, appearing to be shocked by the question.

"What about Michael Ghant? Are you working for him?"

"Sascha, I'm very confused right now. Where is all this coming from?"

"It's coming from the fact that I know you, Dr. Benedict, are full of shit."

"I know you have been…"

"No, it's not that. It's actually the report I received from my private investigator on you."

The color drained from the doctor's face, and he stood up and walked over to stare out of his office window.

"What do you know?" he asked nervously.

"I know that you have been married before, and one of those marriages was to a prior patient. I don't get it. Why lie to me about a dead fiancée?"

"I'm sorry I lied to you."

"I don't want your apology; I want an explanation."

The room was silent for what felt like an eternity. Sascha started to think that Dr. Benedict would offer no explanation when he finally started to speak.

"I didn't mean for this to happen, Sascha," Dr. Benedict

said as he began to pace, nervously running his fingers through his hair. "I swear to you that I have never met your Gina or Michael, but I did follow the trial, and I fell in love with you from afar. I saw your pictures on the cover of newspapers and in magazines, and I watched your court testimony. I was in awe. A fan. I read your books, and I knew you were the one for me. Of course, it was all fantasy for me. I didn't think I had a chance with you or that we would ever really meet in person. Then one day you called my office for an appointment, and I knew I should have declined you as a patient, but it seemed like fate. Deep down I hoped you were this horrible person, deserving of everything that had happened to you, so I could get over you. But you weren't this terrible person. You were more beautiful and wonderful than I had ever imagined."

The words were a lot to take in for Sascha.

"Do you hear yourself? I mean, as a psychiatrist, do you really hear yourself? You need to get some psychological help, and you definitely should not be seeing patients."

"You're right," Dr. Benedict said as he sat back down in his chair and put his face in his hands.

"Why did you pursue Anna Green?"

"Because I wanted to be closer to you. Because I am in love with you," Dr. Benedict said softly as tears filled his eyes.

"How are you any better than Michael when you have been manipulating and grooming me this whole time?" Sascha asked, but Dr. Benedict continued to avoid making eye contact with her. Standing up in frustration, Sascha grabbed her purse. "You are not mentally healthy. Please get help and do not attempt to contact me again," Sascha stated as she shook her head in disgust, and then she left his office. That afternoon she called to report him to the state medical board.

CHAPTER 6

$\mathcal{A}$rriving home from her meeting with Dr. Benedict, Sascha felt anxious and filled with dread. She had texted Devon earlier to tell him she was on her way home, knowing she needed to tell him about filing a report against the doctor, but she had not received a response, which was unusual. Sascha decided to pop her head into Devon's office to let him know she was back. Opening the door she was surprised to see the beautiful Delilah sitting on his desk in a low-cut top, her long hair flowing, and the pair laughing.

Sascha felt her face go red from anger and fear. Devon looked up as she stood there in the doorway and stood up himself and walked over to her.

"Hey, beautiful, where have you been?" Devon asked, planting a quick kiss on her lips.

"At an appointment with Dr. Benedict. I texted you earlier about it," Sascha said, attempting to hide her emotions.

"Hmm, I don't remember any texts from you," Devon replied and started looking around the room. "Now that I think about it, I haven't seen my phone all morning. Delilah, please see if you can locate my phone. It's usually at the same spot on my desk."

"Of course," Delilah said as she hopped off the desk, and Sascha eyed her intensely.

Devon's phone was located moments later on the far side of the room, under a small stack of papers, and was powered off.

"That's weird," he stated as Delilah handed him his phone.

"It sure is," Sascha responded and excused herself.

Sascha decided to wait until after dinner and Danielle had been put to bed for the night before discussing Dr. Benedict with Devon. When Sascha shared the news about Dr. Benedict with Devon, he was furious, both at her and at the doctor. "I thought we agreed to have no more secrets between us." Devon's green eyes flared at Sascha as his anger ignited.

Sascha poured them both a glass of wine and followed her husband to the library so they could sit and talk, as they did every night after dinner.

"I wouldn't exactly call this a secret. Yes, I have suspected him for some time, but I had no actual proof of anything really until recently," she replied sweetly, but she could see from the expression on her husband's face that he was not buying it.

The transition from the kitchen to the library was stark. The library was chilly. Sascha sat down on the couch and pulled a throw blanket over her legs as she watched Devon turn on the gas fireplace. "You should have shared your suspicions about him with me." Devon was facing away from her, but she could tell from his frosty tone that he was not going to let the matter go easily.

"Okay, you're right. I deliberately withheld my suspicions from you because I knew what you would say."

With a healthy fire roaring, Devon came and sat next to

Sascha on the couch and took a sip of his wine. "And what would I have said?"

"You would have told me to stop seeing him. But I was not ready to do that yet. I was getting better. My nightmares were less frequent, my anxiety was under control, and to be honest, I did not quite trust my instincts anymore. What if I was wrong about him?"

"Your instincts are fine," Devon said as he pulled Sascha into his arms, and she snuggled up to him. "It's your beauty and sweetness and kindness that are the problem."

"What does that mean?" Sascha exclaimed as she immediately sat up and glared at her husband.

"I now realize I am going to have to spend the next fifty years of my life fighting off other men because you're utterly irresistible and addictive," Devon said as he pulled her back into his arms.

"Is that going to be a problem?" Sascha teased, and she started kissing his neck.

"I will fight them with relish, my love, because I am never letting you go," Devon said as he ran his hands over Sascha's full breasts. Gone was the anger from Devon's eyes, and in its place was desire. That night Devon and Sascha made love on the library floor in the amber light of a roaring fire, exploring each other's bodies and reaching heights of pleasure that lingered on for hours.

Cuddled on a large, lush area rug and wrapped in multiple blankets, the couple enjoyed the feel of their damp, bare skin touching as their breathing slowed and euphoria surrounded them.

"I was thinking we could go up to our Orcas Island home for a week or so. Think you can squeeze it into your schedule?" Devon asked as he kissed Sascha's shoulder.

"My schedule? Mr. Montague, you are the busy businessman, always on the go, and I am the writer who can work from just about anywhere. I think this is a question for your-self," Sascha stated.

"I thought I was doing better with being home more," Devon said, and Sascha could hear the hurt in his voice.

"You are doing so much better, and I thank you for that, but I'm greedy. I just cannot get enough of you," Sascha said as she captured his mouth and rolled over on top of Devon. "Ready for round two?" she asked as she straddled her husband, but no answer was needed.

Days later the Montagues, along with Sascha's personal assistant, Tatum, Devon's personal assistant, Delilah, Matt, Tom, and Lena all traveled by private plane, piloted by Devon, to the family's Orcas Island home. Orcas Island is the largest of the San Juan Islands in the northern Pacific coast and was considered part of Washington State.

The home was grand with a 365-degree view of the ocean and boasted over six thousand square feet of home on a single level, with a large main bedroom suite, eight guest bedrooms, and a two-bedroom guest house, which besties Tatum and Lena requested to share.

Sascha's father, John, along with her stepmother, Maggie, her younger sister, Sabrina, and best friend, Cate, would all be arriving the following day by ferry from Seattle. Both Sabrina and Cate had to work, and John and Maggie were just getting over the flu, so the extra day to recover was needed. Sascha's stepbrother, Christian, and his fiancée, Yvonne, were also expected to take a break from Christian's congressional campaign trail and join the family for a day or two.

Sascha was excited to have the family together, even Christian, despite their complicated relationship. Christian was the younger brother of Colin, Sascha's college sweet-heart who tragically died nearly fifteen years ago in a hit-and-run accident that went unsolved for years. Gina

Campbell revealed herself as the culprit over a decade later while she held Sascha at gunpoint. With the truth finally revealed, Maggie, Colin's mother, and Christian both came back into Sascha's life. While Maggie and John, Sascha's father, fell in love and got married, Christian revealed his secret love for Sascha the night before their parents' wedding.

Christian was young, good looking, and an up-and-coming politician who was also engaged to marry Yvonne Diadore, a wealthy heiress who bared a striking resemblance to Sascha. He was very open about his feelings for Sascha and told her he would leave Yvonne or any other woman if he knew he had a chance with Sascha. It was an uncomfortable conversation for Sascha to have with her stepbrother, and while she accepted how Christian felt about her, she told him nothing would ever happen between the two of them. Although they had agreed to never speak of the subject again, everyone in their inner circle knew about Christian's feelings for Sascha except their parents, and they all planned to keep it that way.

Arriving at their island estate, Sascha immediately felt like she was on vacation. Although their San Francisco home was her dream home and sat overlooking cliffs and the Pacific Ocean, the island estate was constructed and decorated to resemble an island resort. Walking into the residence, Sascha admired the beauty and elegance of their second home and appreciated the indoor-outdoor living offered with walls of collapsible windows surrounding the home.

As the entourage entered the home, Sascha smiled, pleased at how perfect it was. In preparation for their visit, Sascha gave the house manager very specific instructions for fresh floral arrangements to be placed throughout the house, the type of food and snacks to be stocked in the main house and guest house, as well as room assignments and the personalized gifts she wanted placed in each guest's room.

While everyone found their room and settled in, Sascha continued to stand in the middle of the family room. Looking around she started to feel her anxiety creeping in. Standing there, staring out the massive windows, she realized that someone on the outside of the house could just as easily be looking in at her. She suddenly felt exposed. Biting her lip hard, Sascha silently cursed. She hated how Michael had done this to her. Hearing footsteps behind her, she felt her husband wrap his arms around her waist.

"Don't worry, darling. We can close all the windows, drop down all the window covers, or turn on blackout mode whenever you feel like it. Okay?"

Sascha nodded her head and then turned around to face her husband. "Thank you."

Devon took Sascha's face in his hands and stared deep into her golden-brown eyes before leaning in to cover her lips with his. The soft caress of his mouth over hers made Sascha melt into her husband's arms. Devon wrapped his arms around Sascha and pulled her body tightly against his, which made her feel safe and protected.

"Excuse me, ma'am, I hate to interrupt, but someone is looking for their mother."

Devon and Sascha turned to find Danielle giggling and running toward them. Devon bent down and scooped up their daughter into his arms and planted a kiss on her cheek.

"Thank you, Lena. Please get yourself settled in the guest house and enjoy the home. We will see you after dinner," Sascha informed the nanny.

The Orcas Island estate had its own staff, including a private chef, two housekeepers, and a house manager who saw to all their needs. Sascha adored being at the home because it always felt like a true vacation, although she still planned to write for a few hours each day. Devon also planned to take business calls and meetings in the mornings, but they both agreed to be free for family time and each other no later than noon each day.

Sascha loved hosting friends and family and had events planned for each day for their entire group. There would be boat rides, sailing, fishing, whale watching, in-town shopping, movie nights, and barbecues. The property boasted a hangar, which housed two of Devon's planes, a dock with a speedboat and sailboat, a large heated pool, a game room, and a home movie theater. Best of all the home had an in-home spa area complete with a sauna, an outdoor ten-person hot tub, massage tables, and manicure and pedicure stations. And Sascha's favorite room in the house was their well-equipped home gym, which was perfect since both she and Devon loved to exercise.

Sascha planned to bring in technicians to provide beauty treatments and services to her guests throughout their stay. The group would have plenty to entertain them, or they could choose to just do nothing and relax. Either way Sascha would just be happy to have her family there spending time together.

Day one was kept simple and relaxing for the Montagues. They spent the afternoon exploring their property with their daughter. With two hours of sunlight remaining in the day, Devon, Sascha, and Danielle walked down to their dock and collected rocks before going down to their private beach area to make sandcastles and collect seashells. After a while Danielle started to get tired and ornery, which told her parents it was time to call it a night on their excursion. Arriving back at the home to clean up before dinner, Sascha saw a car stopped at the gate at the end of their drive.

"Do you know who that is?" Sascha asked Devon as she lifted up her sunglasses, hoping to see better into the car.

"No idea. Probably just a tourist or somebody who's lost, but I'm going to go check it out," he responded, and then he said he would meet her back at the house as he started off in the direction of the gate. Sascha spotted Matt walking toward the gate as well and felt better that Devon would not be approaching the car alone.

In the meantime Sascha walked back up to the house, holding Danielle's hand with one hand and a bucket full of their rocks and seashells in the other. It was dinnertime for Danielle and then off to bed for her. While Lena took Danielle to wash up, Sascha went to the kitchen to prepare her daughter's plate. As she chatted with the chef, who was preparing that night's dinner, she suddenly heard familiar voices coming from the other room. Excusing herself, she followed the voices and found her sister and best friend standing in the foyer. Excited to see them, Sascha yelled in happiness and ran over to them to offer welcoming hugs.

"What are you two doing here? I thought you weren't coming until tomorrow."

"We decided to play hooky from work today and come up early to surprise you," Cate said as she and Sabrina looked at one another and laughed.

"Well, I'm so happy you did. I have missed you both," Sascha said, and the three women stood there catching up.

When Lena brought Danielle back out for her dinner, Danielle was greeted with hugs and kisses from both her auntie and Cate, before being led off by her dad to the dining room. Sascha took that opportunity to show the women to their rooms and provide them a quick tour of the home, before being located by Devon. He informed her that dinner was ready to be served when she was ready, and Danielle had been put to bed for the night. Sascha was famished but needed to freshen up and change after being down on the beach earlier. When Sascha came out of her room fifteen minutes later, she found Delilah lurking in the hall.

"Did you need something, Delilah?" Sascha asked, always cautious in her presence.

"No, ma'am. I think I just got turned around. I am trying to find my way out to the guest house to join Tatum and Lena for dinner," Delilah said with a sweet smile that was not working on Sascha.

"Down that hall and to the right, and you will find a side door. Exit that door and just follow the lit path down to the guest house."

Delilah thanked Sascha and started off down the hall. Sascha watched the woman until she was out of sight, continuing to eye her with suspicion. The more time Sascha spent around Delilah, the less she trusted her. Tatum felt the same way, which was why she invited Delilah to join her and Lena for dinner that evening. The plan was for the women to put Delilah at ease and see if they could get her to open up and learn more about her. It was a long shot because Delilah was usually guarded and standoffish, but it was worth a shot to find out if she was another enemy in their midst or just an ambitious woman trying to snag a wealthy man. Either way Sascha was having none of it.

Dinner that night was just what Sascha needed. Her favorite people were there, and the vibe was light and fun. Sabrina talked about the new guy she was dating, which was always an interesting topic as Sabrina seemed to bore of men rather quickly. Matt had been invited to join them for dinner but declined, likely because of Sabrina's presence. It had been over a year since they had broken up, but there still seemed to be tension between the two.

Sascha would love to see them get back together, but she knew her sister was not open to hearing that from her. Cate, on the other hand, was always one to speak her mind, and she had no qualms about bringing the topic up.

"Not that I'm saying you need to be in a relationship, Brina, but how are you not at least friends with benefits with Matt? I mean, have you seen him? He's so hot!" Cate said, and Sascha chuckled at the statement.

"Matt and I are good, but we're just friends, and trust me, there are no lingering feelings between us. Any weirdness you're detecting is not because of me."

Sascha eyed her sister with an unspoken question on her lips.

"So you don't mind if I sleep with him, then?"

"Cate!" Sascha chided her friend in disapproval.

"What? You know it's not like I'm going to do it, but mmm, I would love to. But alas, girl code blah blah blah."

"Sharing is caring," Sabrina responded.

As the women erupted in laughter, Devon took a sip of his wine and looked at his wife with a facial expression that said, "Get me out of here." Sascha winked at her husband and smiled. Devon was always a trouper, but having grown up as an only child, he was not used to being around a group of bantering women. Deciding to change the subject as dessert was served, Sascha went over the week's itinerary.

"Sascha, you are always the hostess with the mostest, but I think I may need a vacation from my vacation by the time the week is done," Cate said.

"Nope. These are planned but suggested activities. There will be eight of us, and I just want to make sure there is always something for everyone to do, but my feelings will not be hurt if you choose to sleep in or lie by the pool instead of going out fishing."

"Don't worry, I will not be missing out on shopping or spa time," Cate said.

"I didn't think you would," Sascha teased.

CHAPTER 7

The morning of day two started off perfect. Sascha was awoken by her lusty husband for delicious morning lovemaking. Afterward the couple went down to their dock and enjoyed watching the sunrise. The morning was chilly, but the couple was wrapped in a blanket, and they each enjoyed a thermos of piping-hot coffee. Just as Sascha and Devon were walking back up to the house, the yoga instructor Sascha had requested was arriving to teach a sunrise yoga class. Devon, having no interest in yoga, departed for the home gym, while Sascha took the instructor down to their beach area. Sascha was not expecting anyone else to show up to the class but was pleasantly surprised to see both Sabrina and Tatum dressed and ready for yoga.

The morning yoga was invigorating and was followed by a short meditation session. By the time Sascha returned to the main house, she was on cloud nine. Walking into the home, she smelled breakfast, and her stomach growled in response. Entering the breakfast room, Sascha found Cate loading up a plate with potatoes, eggs, bacon, and fruit.

"Good morning, Cate," Sascha said sweetly as she walked over to give her friend a quick hug and grabbed a plate.

"You missed a beautiful sunrise this morning and some amazing yoga," Sascha said, and she took a bite of her bacon.

"I thought about getting up, but I was sleeping too damn good," Cate replied, and she sipped her coffee.

"Oh good! I'm glad you got the rest you needed."

"Morning, Cate," Sabrina said as she entered the dining room, carrying a smoothie she had the chef make for her breakfast.

"Yuck, you and your smoothies, Sabrina. I wish I had your discipline," Cate teased, and she took a big bite of her buttered toast.

Sascha rolled her eyes as the two women got into a discussion about nutrition and fasting. Both Sabrina and Cate were naturally thin women. Sabrina, at five-foot-two, always maintained her petite frame, and Cate at five-foot-eleven had struggled in the past to gain weight. Meanwhile Sascha had to watch what she ate and how much she ate, and she worked out regularly to maintain her fifty-pound weight loss after her divorce from her first husband, Lucas.

"Okay, so what are we doing today?" Sabrina asked, and she popped a grape in her mouth.

"I have to do some writing this morning but will be available after eleven today. Dad and Maggie will be arriving around 3:00 p.m. In the meantime you two can enjoy the pool, have a massage, get facials, or do manicures and pedicures. Just let me know what you want," Sascha said.

"I want it all," Cate responded.

"Of course you do," Sascha responded, and she laughed and started texting the service providers on her phone.

As Sascha went into her island office to write, her guests enjoyed pampering that morning. Sascha was not too envious because she planned on getting a massage and manicure that afternoon with Maggie once she arrived. Maggie was Sascha's new stepmother and one of her favorite people in the world. No one could ever replace her deceased mother in her life or in her heart, but Sascha could not have chosen a better mate for her father or a better addition to their family.

At noon Sascha, Devon, and Danielle enjoyed lunch by the pool and afterward got in and splashed around until Danielle was tuckered out and ready for her afternoon nap. While Danielle napped, and before her parents arrived, Sascha and Devon took advantage of their alone time and made love with fervor and took a quick nap themselves. They were on vacation too after all.

By the time her father and Maggie arrived, Sascha was up and about, had fresh flowers placed in their bedroom, had two large charcuterie boards available for afternoon snacks, and was working with the chef on that night's menu. Seeing the two of them together always made Sascha smile. Her father and Maggie were so happy and in love, and she found their happiness contagious.

The grandparents greeted everyone but were mostly excited to see their granddaughter, Danielle. And their granddaughter was just as happy to see them, running to them when she saw them walk into the room. Sascha put an emotional hand to her heart, holding back tears as she looked around the room at those she loved, gathered, talking, and laughing. After grabbing snack plates, Sascha showed her father and Maggie to their room.

"Sascha, this is absolutely stunning," Maggie said as she stopped and stared at the beautiful views from the floor-to-ceiling windows down the long corridor. "Being out here is like being on your own private island."

"It is. I am so in love with this home and with this island. It's a wonderful and peaceful place, and I cannot wait to take you both around it and show you all it has to offer."

Sascha left her father and Maggie in their room to settle in and returned to the kitchen area. Tonight's menu was to be surf and turf, something for everyone. Both Devon and her father were big meat eaters, while Sascha and Cate rarely ate red meat, and Sabrina was a pescatarian. After dinner Sascha planned for a movie night. Each guest had a voting card in their room to pick the evening's movie choice. All the movie options were classics, lighthearted, and usually crowd pleasers. The movie with the most votes would decide what they watched for movie night.

The group enjoyed spending time together and got along well. There was rarely conflict, disagreements, or awkwardness among them. Sascha knew she needed to appreciate this time because once Christian and Yvonne arrived, the entire group dynamic would change, and not likely for the better.

Christian and Yvonne arrived late on day two while the group was singing along to a classic movie as Sabrina and Tatum acted out a "Pink Ladies" scene. Both Christian and Yvonne were tired and decided to settle in for the night after saying their hellos to the group. Sascha showed them to their room, and after having a plate of snacks and drinks sent to the pair, Sascha returned to the home theater. Sascha had fun and enjoyed the evening, but she also kept her eye on sneaky Delilah who seemed to be observing the group, especially her.

After Tatum's report of Delilah from the previous evening, Sascha had no doubt that Delilah was up to no good and had an agenda. Delilah had asked Tatum and Lena a lot of personal questions, mostly about Sascha, but she also asked about the Montagues' marriage, Sascha's mental health, and about any upcoming travel plans for Sascha. Tatum was certain that Delilah was after Devon, which was completely possible, but Sascha could not rule out Michael's hand in this somehow.

While Devon would want to fire Delilah immediately if he even suspected she was involved with Michael, Sascha decided this might be the perfect opportunity to flush him out and feed him false information via his little spy. And if Tatum was correct, and Delilah was just an opportunistic witch who wanted to steal her man, Sascha was ready to teach her a lesson. As Sascha leaned back in her seat, and Devon put his arm around her, she felt eyes on her. Turning to her left, Sascha caught Delilah's gaze, and the woman quickly turned away.

Sascha was drained by the time she went to bed that night. It had been a long day, and as much as she loved hosting, it was demanding and exhausting. Checking in on Danielle, whose room was right across from theirs, the Montagues found their little girl curled up and sleeping deeply. Sascha checked the monitor for Danielle's room and set the internal window and door alarms for her daughter's room. Their home was high tech and high security, but this was the first night Sascha had ever used the individual room alarm system since they had purchased the home.

Devon gave her an odd look.

"Lindbergh baby," Sascha said, and left the room.

ON DAY three at the island, Sascha stopped doing her sunrise yoga to wave at Captain Nyles, the boat captain who had just arrived to take the men of their group out on a daylong fishing trip. Captain Nyles was an Orcas Island native, a military veteran, and a retired ferry boat captain. He often referred to himself as an old salty dog, but Sascha found the old man charming, and she knew he and her father would get along great.

Sascha's father loved fishing and was an expert fisherman, and while neither Devon nor Christian were experienced fishermen, they were getting better according to her dad. Sascha's father, John, had been the best dad when she was growing up and always made his daughters feel special and loved, but Sascha always wondered if deep down he wished he also had a son or two.

Sascha knew Devon enjoyed spending time with her father, which warmed her heart. While Christian was still developing his relationship with Sascha's dad, his new stepfather, she could tell Christian was happy to have him in his life. Both Devon and Christian had grown up without fathers in their lives. Devon was fatherless by desertion, and Christian was fatherless by death.

As the group of men came out to meet Captain Nyles, they all waved at Sascha and promised to bring back plenty of fish from their trip. Freshly caught salmon was expected to be on the menu for dinner that evening.

While the men spent the day fishing, the women went into town for shopping and lunch. Sascha loved the wonderful boutique stores on the island and was sure the group of women would love them as well. Sascha, Sabrina, Cate, Maggie, Yvonne, and Danielle enjoyed the perfect weather as they walked from shop to shop, buying knick-knacks and sampling food and sweets. By the time they stopped for lunch, Sascha was not very hungry and just enjoyed a light salad. At the end of lunch, Danielle started to get fussy, and Sascha knew it was nap time for her little one and decided to head back but encouraged the rest of the group to stay and continue sightseeing. Maggie, still slightly under the weather, returned with Sascha and Danielle, while the rest of the group went off for wine tasting at a wine shop.

Sascha and Maggie always enjoyed spending time together, and conversation on the way back to the house was light and easy, while a tired Danielle was not easy. Sascha arrived back at the home ready for sleep herself, and after putting Danielle down for her nap, she crawled onto her bed for a quick power nap.

Hours later Sascha woke to a dark room and hands caressing her body. She recognized her husband's shower-wash scent and his lips as he kissed her neck. Damp hands pulled her top over her head and slid her shorts down her legs before Devon's naked body quickly covered Sascha's. She ran her fingers through his wet hair as his mouth found his way down her body. Sascha had intended to ask how the trip went, but her mind went blank as her husband showed her how much he had missed her that day.

DAY four of Sascha's vacation started off peaceful. Sascha decided she would not work at all that day but just relax and enjoy the perfect weather they were having with her family and friends. Christian and Yvonne were leaving later in the day, but the rest of the group would remain for the rest of the week.

Sitting on the lounge chair, enjoying the sunrays, Sascha watched in joy as Devon played with Danielle in the pool. Danielle giggled and screamed in happiness as her father spun her around, and they splashed one another. Sascha lay back and smiled. She was starting to nod off to sleep when her phone on the side table began to vibrate. Picking up her phone, Sascha saw Devon's name on the caller ID, which was odd considering she was staring right at her husband in the pool.

Sascha reluctantly answered the call. "Hello."

"Oh, how I have missed you and your lovely voice," Michael said on the other line. Sascha's heart began to race. Michael was a tech genius, and hacking and duplicating a phone was child's play for him. Sascha's inner voice told her to calm her nerves. She needed Michael to come out of hiding, and the only way she could do that would be for him to believe she did not hate him. She needed him to think she understood him and was willing to forgive him. Neither of those things were true. Sascha would never understand Michael and could not forgive him for hurting so many people, but he didn't need to know that.

"You've been a bad girl, Sascha. You need to stop searching for me."

"Michael, you have to come back. Clear your name and share your side of the story. Make people understand; otherwise, you will always be on the run. Is that what you want?" Sascha hoped to finally get through to Michael. He was not built for his current lifestyle.

"I want you, that's it. Pretty simple."

Devon noticed Sascha's face on the intense phone call, handed Danielle off to Lena, and started heading her way. Once by her side, he mouthed, *Who is it?* And Sascha quietly told him it was Michael. Devon's face completely changed, and Sascha put her hand up to discourage him from saying anything, but she put the phone call on speaker.

"Sascha dear, I need you to stop looking for me. It's a simple request." Michael's words were cold.

"Michael, I cannot do that."

"Then you will force me to show you how far my reach goes. Don't make me do something I do not want to do to teach you a lesson."

"You would hurt me, Michael?" Sascha asked in a fake, fearful tone.

"Of course not. Never. But others around you won't be given that grace."

"Michael, please…"

"I have to let you go for now, dear, but do enjoy the rest of your day by the pool, and I will be in touch again soon."

As Michael ended the call, Sascha stood up and turned around in circles, searching for any possible sighting of him. She could feel panic setting in and an attack coming on. Devon pulled her into a hug and whispered in her ear, "He's not here. He's not here. He has either hacked into our security cameras, or we have a spy in our midst."

Sascha swallowed hard because she knew both possibilities could be true. Her wonderful vacation came to a screeching halt, and now she just wanted to go back home.

CHAPTER 8

*A*rriving back home from their vacation to Orcas Island, Sascha felt more anxious and stressed than she had in a long time. After her phone call with Michael, she was furious, and while she felt a renewed determination to find him, she also felt terribly vulnerable. And vulnerability was a feeling that never sat well with her. Although Michael was a wanted man on the run, it was clear he was still stalking Sascha, just from afar. He would never give up on wanting her for himself, which was why she needed to find him first, but with Michael's money and his resources, he could possibly run forever.

Sascha was happy to be home but needed to find a way to control the anxiety attack she felt coming on. Devon walked in the door behind her, carrying a sleeping Danielle, while the staff brought in their luggage.

"You look like you might enjoy a run right about now," Devon said, and then he softly kissed her lips before continuing upstairs to put their daughter down.

Devon is right, Sascha thought as she followed him up the

stairs to change into her running clothes. Normally Sascha would run on her treadmill in their home gym, but today she felt like she needed a long run outside in the fresh, salty air to help calm her nerves.

As her husband started prepping dinner in their outdoor kitchen, Sascha asked him if he wanted help before she set off on her run.

"No, but don't be gone for too long. You only have about an hour of light before it's dark out."

"I won't be gone too long. Love you," Sascha responded, before planting a kiss on her husband's cheek.

As Sascha stood in her circular drive, she popped in her earbuds, turned on her music, and put her phone in a secure pocket in her leggings. After taking five minutes to stretch, Sascha started off running in a slow jog. With darkness approaching soon, Sascha decided to avoid the trails in the forest and stuck to the walking trails along the seaside. As Sascha ran, her body began to feel more relaxed and at ease. Sascha normally made plans as she ran. Running was often used to plot out her books and to make her to-do list, but not tonight—tonight she did not want to think at all. The stress and anxiety in her body and mind began to slip away, and she was able to think clearly once again.

Sascha ran until the sun set, and it was nearly dark out. About a half mile from her home, she decided to walk for her cooldown. Sascha took a path that led to the entrance of the forest trails. As she walked, a group of bike riders passed her, and the Swell patrol waved to her as they drove by. Sascha was once again alone when she saw a dark figure exit the forest. The figure was hooded, but Sascha could tell it was a woman. The woman started to walk briskly, and she kept turning around to look behind her, as if she was worried that she was being followed. As the woman kept walking, she pulled out her phone and began furiously texting. Distracted, she did not notice Sascha coming her way until Sascha said, "Good evening."

The hooded figure looked up, startled, and Sascha recognized the woman as her illuminated phone lit her face.

"Marissa, are you all right?" Sascha asked when she saw the woman's face was streaked with black from her makeup running. She was clearly upset and had been crying.

A frightened expression crossed Marissa Tanner's face before a haughty glare quickly replaced it. "I'm fine. I just can't find my stupid dog."

"Oh, okay. Well, would you like for me to help find them?"

"No. He will be fine. A night in the woods will teach him a lesson about running off. I will send my servants out to find him tomorrow."

Hmm, Sascha thought. She did not believe Marissa, but she did not want to argue with the horrible woman.

"Okay, well then, good night," Sascha said, and she decided to run the rest of the way home after all and took off in a jog.

When Sascha returned home, she smelled the grill going and immediately felt her hunger kick in. Walking out to their backyard to let Devon know she was back, Sascha heard a female giggling as she approached and found Delilah standing behind Devon at the grill, asking for cooking tips. Sascha frowned as she recognized Delilah's game instantly and did not like it one bit. Delilah was flirting with Devon, in Sascha's own house. Delilah seemed to have permanently dropped the studious assistant act she put on for them in her London interview, and in her place was a woman with long, flowing hair, tight jeans, and a low-cut top. Sascha's first instinct was to drag her by her hair out the front door and to tell her she was fired, but she knew that was just petty jealousy talking. Delilah was up to no good, that was for sure, but what exactly Sascha did not know. She wanted to keep her around for a little longer to find out, but she was not going to tolerate blatant disrespect.

"I'm back from my run," Sascha interrupted, and Delilah looked up in surprise and moved away from Devon.

"Hey, sweetheart, dinner is almost ready," Devon said as he looked up from the grill, oblivious to the efforts of the temptress standing behind him.

"Sounds good. I'm going to go take a quick shower and will be back down shortly. And, Delilah, I think it's getting pretty late. You should probably get going yourself, yes?" Sascha fixed her eyes on Delilah in a manner that told Delilah that saying no was not an option.

Delilah's eyes flashed annoyance, but a sweet smile made an appearance.

"There's plenty of food. Delilah, you are welcome to join us if you have no other plans," Devon chimed in, not noticing the silent duel taking place between the two women.

"No, thank you, sir. I had better get going. You two have a good night," Delilah said as she hurried back into the house to grab her things.

After Delilah's departure Sascha stared at her husband for a few moments, and there was nothing there. No indication that he was aware of the interaction that had just transpired between his wife and his assistant, nor was he aware that his wife was keeping an extra eye on their interactions. Sascha shook her head and thought, *Men can be so dumb sometimes when it comes to women.* Her husband was completely oblivious to the shenanigans of his new assistant, and with all the other things going on in their life at the time, Sascha decided not to bring up the issue and ruin their night.

When Sascha sat down to dinner that night, she just wanted to enjoy her food and have a nice glass of wine and good conversation with her husband. And, of course, hot sex in the library—that always seemed to follow dinner these days.

CHAPTER 9

hile Sascha continued working on her new book, a television series was being made based off her earlier books in the series, and filming was nearly complete. Sascha and Tatum had visited the television set a couple of times over the past few months, and she was proud and excited with how the writer and directors were handling her work.

Sascha had an open invitation to the television set but worried that her constant presence would be a distraction, so she decided to visit only once a month. She trusted Marcus Winters, the show's creator and primary director, and his vision for bringing her stories to life. The wrap party was being held the following day, and Sascha, Cate, and Tatum would be attending it in Vancouver, Canada. Sascha breathed a sigh of relief that filming seemed to go smoothly, but Marcus warned her that the real work happened postproduction, especially with this project as it required quite a lot of special effects.

While Sascha packed she sat on a bench in her closet, looking around and trying to decide what to wear for the wrap party. She had a closet full of clothes and shoes, most of them in black, and some items with pops of color, but she struggled to make a decision.

"Aw, is someone pouting because they can't decide what to wear from their department-store closet?" Sascha looked up to find Cate standing there, and she burst out laughing. She had missed her acerbic friend last year and was so glad to have her back to her unfiltered, sarcastic self.

"Well, what are you wearing for the wrap party?" Sascha asked Cate, and she saw her looking through the hanging clothes.

"No idea, that's why I'm here. My plan is to raid your closet."

"Have at it, but most of my clothes are probably too big for you."

"Not likely, but I am looking for something classy and comfortable, which you always have plenty of," Cate replied as she affectionately squeezed Sascha's hand and began pillaging the closet.

After nearly an hour of trying on outfits and finding the perfect one for each of them, they sat on the closet area rug and ate from pints of ice cream.

"I think I want you and Devon to adopt me and let me live in this fabulous closet."

The women laughed and talked for the rest of the night.

THE TRIP to Vancouver was a first for Sascha. She was beyond excited to attend the final day of filming for the Coven of Plumvale series and to attend the wrap party with the stars and crew. It was nearly over a year and a half ago that Sascha had optioned her book rights to famed director Marcus Winters and his production company and entrusted him with her beloved characters. From what she had seen on set, the fierce magical vibes from her books would be on full display on screen.

Arriving at their beautiful mountain hotel, Sascha bundled up as the weather was chillier than expected for late summer. Sascha, along with Cate and Tatum, quickly deposited her bags in her room and went back down to the lobby to meet up with Matt and their driver. As Sascha walked through the lobby, she felt eyes following her. When Cate arrived Sascha commented on people staring at her and making her feel uncomfortable.

"They're staring at you because you look hot," Cate commented as she buttoned her jacket.

"I agree. You're looking like a MILF," Tatum teased.

"See? I told you so. Matt would agree, too, if he didn't think Devon would break his neck for checking out his wife," Cate said, and Matt looked away uncomfortably.

"Car is here," Matt said in an awkward mumble as he motioned for the women to head toward the glass doors.

As Sascha started walking, she caught her reflection in a mirror and had to admire her ensemble. Her shoulder-length curly hair was down and voluminous and streaked with golden strands from the summer sun. She wore fitted jeans, with cognac-colored thigh-high boots, and a belted camel-colored cashmere sweater that flattered her trim waist. *Hmm, maybe I am a MILF,* Sascha thought, and she chuckled to herself and walked with confidence out the hotel lobby doors.

The drive out to the set location was only a half hour, and it went by fast as Sascha chatted with Tatum and Cate and enjoyed the scenic landscape. When Sascha walked onto the set, the crew clapped for her. She was completely taken aback and brought to tears. After a few moments, Sascha found her place behind Marcus, and he yelled, "Action!" She held her breath as the main character flew up into the rafters, and Marcus yelled, "Cut!" and season one of the Coven of Plumvale wrapped.

A teary-eyed Tatum pulled Sascha into a hug and told her how proud she was of her. Tatum's words meant a lot to Sascha. Tatum Chee had been with Sascha for over four years and was more than just a personal assistant—she was family. Tatum was brilliant and spunky and currently sporting blue hair on her faux hawk. She was the perfect personal assistant, and Sascha would keep her forever, but Sascha knew she had so much more potential. Sascha also knew Tatum was not someone you could push. She had to do things in her own time.

Sascha and her group headed back to their hotel to get ready for the wrap party later that evening. The party was expected to be a large event with a red carpet, press, and an interview panel. Sascha was excepting a long but fun night. After exiting her shower, she threw on a bathrobe and did a video call with Devon and Danielle. Danielle was not happy that her mommy was not there, but Sascha promised both her loves she would be home the following day.

The wrap party was a wonderful way to end the amazing experience of Sascha's first book being turned into a television show. The night was filled with speeches of appreciation, followed by lots of great food, drinks, and fantastic music. Sascha danced until her feet hurt, and while she mingled and partied with the cast and crew members, she noticed Cate and Marcus spent most of the night talking at a table. Marcus was not at all Cate's type, but Sascha had no intentions of mentioning that fact to Cate. After Cate's nightmare marriage to Michael, thanks to Sascha's matchmaking, Sascha would not dare to interfere in Cate's love life again.

CHAPTER 10

"*L*ook what I drew, Mommy," Danielle exclaimed as she held up a picture to show Sascha. Sascha had no idea what she was looking at, but as far as she was concerned, it was as perfect as a Monet.

"Beautiful! I love it!" Sascha said as her daughter beamed with pride. "Will you draw another?" Sascha requested, and her little girl continued to sketch in her book while she lay on her parents' bed.

A soft tap at Sascha's open bedroom door drew her attention.

"Excuse me, ma'am, are you ready for me to take your bags down to the car?"

Sascha looked up to see Ben, a member of the household staff, standing at her bedroom door. Devon walked out of their bathroom with his toiletry bag in hand and dropped it into his open suitcase.

"Morning, Ben," Devon said in a chipper voice.

As Sascha greeted Ben, she told him which bags were ready to be taken down and directed him to also grab Danielle's bag, which was still in her room.

The family was going out of town for the weekend to attend Christian and Yvonne's grand wedding at her parents' Massachusetts compound. Though Sascha had never been to the home, she had seen photos in several architect and real estate magazines, and it was stunning, and she was interested to see it in person. The guest list consisted of just five hundred of their closest friends and family, and it was sure to be an intimate affair, Sascha thought as she rolled her eyes.

"What's that face for?" Devon asked as he observed his wife.

"I'm not looking forward to this weekend. I don't like Yvonne, and she does not like me, and add to that knowing how Christian feels about me, it makes for an uncomfortable event. Plus, all the announcements and events planned keep referring to me as his sister, which is kind of true, I suppose, but it just makes everything feel so incestuous."

"Yeah, it's creepy." Devon's agreement with Sascha's words was unexpected.

"Devon, you're not helping."

"Listen, I think it's all by design. Yvonne knows Christian is in love with you, and she wants to make both of you feel guilty and grossed out by any lustful thoughts that may exist."

"Okay, so she's an evil genius. Well, if that was her plan, it is definitely working on me, but I doubt Christian is affected by her choice of words at all."

"He has spent most of his adult life knowing you as the woman his deceased brother was going to marry. If that information did not change his heart and desires, then nothing will."

Sascha nodded her head and took a deep breath. Nothing was changing Christian's mind, and this weekend was likely to be one of the most awkward of her life.

Sabrina joined the Montagues on their private jet to the

East Coast, while Sascha's father, John, and stepmother, Maggie, went ahead days earlier to attend prewedding festivities in Massachusetts. Sascha was happy that she had not been expected to attend any events leading up to the wedding weekend, which was likely Yvonne's preference, and Sascha appreciated that.

Once the plane hit cruising altitude, Sabrina got up out of her seat and went over to chat with the Montagues.

"So how excited is everyone for this weekend?" Sabrina asked Devon and Sascha with a glint of mischief in her eyes.

Devon refused to take the bait, but Sascha could not help herself.

"Oh, we're super excited, dear Brina. In fact, I cannot wait to have another sister," Sascha responded, rolling her eyes at her sister.

Sabrina laughed hysterically and went back to her seat, while Sascha waved for the flight attendant to bring her a prosecco. Sascha leaned back in her seat and closed her eyes in an effort to bring down her anxiety.

"It will be over before you know it, my love." Devon's whispered words had a calming effect on Sascha, and she was able to relax.

It was Friday morning, and while Sascha normally loved a three-day weekend, she was not looking forward to spending the long holiday weekend with Yvonne and her family. The Diadores were old money, and if Yvonne was any indication of how the rest of her family would be, Sascha was expecting loads of snobbery and airs of superiority. Although Sascha liked nice things, she never really cared much about money and did not place value on people based on net worth, unlike many others she had met since joining the high society.

Arriving at Yvonne's family compound on Martha's Vineyard was an experience in itself. Much like Orcas Island, Martha's Vineyard was an island known for its affluent summer residents. Martha's Vineyard was to be reached by boat, ferry, or plane. The Montagues flew by private jet to the scenic location to attend what many were calling the societal wedding of the year.

As the Montagues, along with Sabrina and their staff, were driven from the hangar to the family's main house, Sascha enjoyed the views. Although she lived on the coast, with cliffs right outside her back door, Sascha always appreciated all ocean views and the unique beauty offered at each location. Breathing in the salty air, she noticed the Atlantic Ocean's air smelled slightly different from the Pacific Ocean. Sascha also noticed a lighthouse at the end of the property, which she planned to visit the minute she had the opportunity to do so.

The car stopped in front of a massive, beautiful, white, Cape Cod–style home with two house staff members waiting there to greet them.

Oh, how lovely, Sascha thought. She had always loved the look of Cape Cod homes. As the man opened her door and helped her out of the car, Sascha realized the weekend would be filled with pomp and circumstance. Though not surprised that Yvonne would put on quite the show for her guests, Sascha was not looking forward to a wedding weekend full of formalities.

The house manager appeared and informed the group of the sleeping arrangements. Sascha, Devon, and Danielle would be shown to one of the private guest cottages on the property, while Sabrina would be sleeping in the main house, and Lena would sleep in the staff quarters. Sascha quickly looked to Lena, who chuckled as she grabbed her bag and said she would be fine. As a young lady stepped forward to take Lena to her room, a young man pulled up on a golf cart and started loading the Montagues' bags onto it.

"Umm, that one is mine." Sabrina stepped in and grabbed

her bag off the cart. Making eye contact with her sister, she smirked and said, "See you later, sissy," as she, too, was escorted off to her room.

Devon, Danielle, and Sascha all loaded into the golf cart, and off they went to their cottage. Arriving at their cottage a few minutes later, Sascha noticed there were several other cottages in the same area of the property and that they all had name placards and varied in size. Sascha's cottage's name was Her Majesty, and it appeared to be the largest of the cottages. The staff member unloaded their bags and placed them in the cottage. He gave instructions on how to reach the staff if they needed anything and wished them an enjoyable stay before he was off.

A large bench with throw pillows sat outside the lovely cottage. Sascha knew she would find herself seated there a few times over the next couple of days. Walking into the cottage, Sascha was pleasantly surprised. The cottage was charming. The cottage emulated the Cape Cod style inside and out. With two bedrooms to accommodate the couple and their young child, the cottage perfectly fit their needs, and it appeared that the small details were considered. There was a large bowl filled with fruit in a small kitchenette area, along with a coffee maker, a basket of snacks, a few bottles of her favorite wine, and a mini fridge that contained milk, juice, and Sascha's preferred creamer.

"Yvonne did good. I think your new sister-in-law went out of her way to make us feel welcomed here," Devon said as he opened up a package of crackers for Danielle to snack on.

"She did indeed. I will be sure to thank her," Sascha said in response, but she felt differently. She knew these arrangements were not likely Yvonne's doing but Christian's. Christian knew Sascha's favorite wine and coffee, he knew her favorite colors, and he knew that she would want a cottage facing the lighthouse.

The weekend's itinerary sat in a picture frame on the kitchenette counter. Every moment up to the wedding reception on Sunday afternoon was planned out in detail.

Once the Montagues were settled in, they decided to sit outside on the bench and enjoy the view. With guests spread out across the property, communication was coming in the form of group texts. Both Sascha's and Devon's phones chimed at the same time, stating dinner would be served at the main house in a half hour. A few moments later, there was a tap at the door. Sascha answered the door and found Lena standing there and the golf cart parked behind her.

"Hello, I am here to take over with Danielle as you two head to dinner," Lena said in a chipper voice.

"Hey, Lena, come on in. I just need to grab my wrap, and we will be heading out," Sascha said as she closed the door behind their nanny. Once the door was closed, Sasha continued, "Okay, Lena, so truth time. How are your accommodations in the 'servants' quarters,' and how are they treating you?"

Sitting down a tray with covered plates, Lena started. "Well, I'm not going to lie—it does all feel a little *Downton Abbey*-ish with the strict separation of guests and staff, but my room, though small, is very nice, and the rest of the staff is friendly and kind. We have already had a great dinner in the staff kitchen, and I have no concerns or complaints."

"That's great to hear. Please let me know if that changes," Sascha responded. Pointing to the tray Lena had sat down, Sascha asked, "Can I assume that's Danielle's dinner?"

"Yes, ma'am. All Danielle's favorites, so I do not believe your little one will have any complaints."

"Awesome, thank you, Lena. We will see you in a couple of hours," Sascha said, and she and Devon gave Danielle kisses and walked out to the golf cart.

While driving to the main house in the golf cart, Sascha

admired the lighthouse as the light beams lit the dark, seaside night. While the driver drove along a well-lit path to the family house, he chatted with Devon about the history of the house and about Martha's Vineyard. Sascha vaguely listened as she enjoyed the cool, damp air on her face.

Pulling up to the main house drive, Sascha found her dad, Maggie, and Christian standing there.

"There's my baby girl," Sascha's dad chimed as he embraced her. Maggie immediately followed with hugs, and then so did Christian. While Sascha lingered in her embraces with her father and Maggie, she quickly left Christian's arms, despite his reluctance to let her go. As the family began to walk inside the home, Maggie fell back and linked her arm with Sascha's.

"We need to talk about Christian later," she whispered, and Sascha nodded but suddenly felt a lump in her throat.

CHAPTER 11

Walking into the Diadore home, Sascha was once again struck by its loveliness. Devon and Sascha were directed to follow a man, who appeared to be a butler, to a great room where the family was enjoying cocktail hour. Entering the room Yvonne's parents immediately walked over and greeted the Montagues.

"It's wonderful to finally meet you," the couple said as they shook hands with Devon and Sascha.

The Diadores were an American legacy family. They were a powerful, wealthy, political stronghold of a family. Two members of their family were current members of Congress, and they boasted a former US president, a former vice president, and three senators. And while their family had had many successes over the years, their family had always been plagued by scandals. There were many claims of adultery and children out of wedlock with mistresses, driving-under-the-influence arrests, accusations of unsavory business practices, a prison sentence for insider trading, and allegations of being involved in the disappearance of a missing young woman who was presumed dead.

Zara Diadore was a kind, quiet woman and looked nothing like her daughter Yvonne. Zara was a tiny woman, in stark contrast to her husband, Bobby, a bear of a man who was loud and boisterous. Sascha quickly noticed that Bobby was a drinker and had a roving eye, as his eyes found her breasts multiple times throughout the evening as he attempted to flirt with her. His flirting did not go unnoticed by neither Devon nor Christian, who both looked annoyed by the man. Sascha was unbothered by the behavior as she often found herself the recipient of unwanted attention from arrogant men who thought they were entitled to have whomever they wanted.

Wanting to leave Bobby Diadore's presence as quickly as possible, Sascha excused herself from the conversation with the elder Diadores and went to meet Yvonne's two sisters, whom Sabrina was currently talking to. With a glass of prosecco in hand, Sascha winked at her husband and walked over to introduce herself to Willa and Francesca, Yvonne's older sisters. The sisters were friendly and funny and appeared to have a great relationship. Both of the sisters wore wedding bands, but neither appeared to have spouses there that night. The ladies chatted and laughed until the dinner bell rang, and the group was ushered into the massive dining room.

There was assigned seating, and as Devon and Sascha took their seats next to one another, they were surrounded by Diadores on all sides, while Sabrina, Maggie, and their dad sat at the far end of the table. Sitting across from the Montagues were Yvonne's younger brother, Alex, and their awful drunk uncle Dante. Sascha tried to ignore them, but they kept pulling her into offensive and sexist conversations she had no interest in. The opinions coming from the two men who had never worked an honest day in their lives made Sascha want to scream, but Devon chuckled under his breath at their comments, calmed her, and made her view them as silly, uninformed men who lacked self-awareness and were not worth her ire.

As the large Italian feast began to be served, Yvonne let her displeasure with the meal be known to all.

"I have to fit into a wedding dress in two days. Why are we serving all these carbs?" Yvonne loudly demanded, turning to her mother.

"I asked for an Italian meal to be served tonight. I thought it would be a nice way to celebrate your family's heritage, and since we are not serving Italian food at the rehearsal dinner tomorrow night or at the wedding reception, I figured it would be a treat for everyone," her mother said.

"Besides, you look great now and will look great on Sunday," Christian said calmly, although Sascha recognized the irritation in his tone.

"Oh of course. What a great idea," Yvonne replied as she took a small serving of pasta.

Sascha was mortified that Yvonne would speak this way to her mother at all but especially in front of the group. Sascha watched Yvonne's sisters make eye contact with one another and roll their eyes at their sister's behavior. None of the Diadores batted an eye or spoke up against the behavior, which told Sascha this was normal behavior for the woman.

The rest of dinner that evening with the Diadore family was pleasant enough. The food and wine were perfection; the people were meh. They were a mixed bag of personalities, and while Sascha liked Yvonne's sisters more than she expected to, she detested her brother and uncle as they were both obnoxious creeps. Happy for dinner to finally be over, Sascha stood up and grabbed Devon's hand to let him know she was ready to go back to their cottage. He smiled down at her with a knowing glint in his eyes. Just as they were ready to say their goodbyes, Maggie walked up to Sascha and asked to chat with her for a few moments.

Maggie and Sascha hung back in the dining room as the rest of the group returned to the great room to enjoy more cocktails. *This family loves to drink*, Sascha thought, but then felt guilty for being so judgmental.

"I'm so excited you all finally made it here," Maggie said, and she breathed a sigh of relief.

"I bet. Your in-laws are a lot." Sascha chuckled.

Maggie nodded her head in agreement but was careful not to speak negatively about the Diadores.

"So what's going on? What did you want to discuss?"

Maggie's body language changed, and she became obviously nervous. "I don't know how to say this or if I should even be discussing this at all," Maggie started, then once again paused.

"Okay, now you are making me nervous."

"I'm sorry. I don't mean to be dramatic, but I cannot keep quiet any longer." Maggie wrung her hands, and Sascha reached out and grabbed her hands in support.

"Just say it," Sascha whispered encouragingly.

"I know Christian is in love with you," Maggie blurted out as her face turned beet red.

"Ah" was all Sascha could manage.

"I don't usually get involved in his personal life, and I would most certainly not presume to tell you what to do, but I love our beautiful new family, and I don't want anything to ruin it."

Sascha nodded in agreement, not sure where the conversation was going.

"I have tried to convince Christian to focus on his future with Yvonne and not let his feelings for you distract him from creating a happy life with her, but as you saw with tonight's display, that is never going to happen. She's awful," Maggie said to Sascha's surprise.

"You and Devon are perfectly matched and so in love that

there is nothing Christian could ever say or do that would change that fact, which is why I ask you to continue to be there for Christian, as a big sister and as a friend. He adores you, but he also trusts you and respects you, and there are not many people in his life I can say that about."

"Of course," Sascha responded, and paused before she continued. "I think Christian and I have an understanding, and as long as he respects the boundaries I have set, we're good."

"Wonderful," Maggie responded as she put a loving hand on Sascha's arm.

"Does Daddy know about this?"

"No, and I think we should keep it that way," Maggie answered, eyeing Sascha expectantly.

"Agreed."

CHAPTER 12

The following day the Diadores' compound was full of events on the water as additional guests arrived for the rehearsal dinner, including Yvonne's bridesmaids and Christian's groomsmen. Some of the wedding guests were staying at a quaint inn not far from the estate, but most were flying in or boating in on the day of the wedding. The Diadores had chartered a ferry to bring their guests across the Vineyard Sound to Martha's Vineyard.

Massive tents were being set up on the far end of the property for the wedding and reception the following day, but today was for fun, relaxing, and the rehearsal dinner. Sascha had no interest in being in the water today, but she did want to explore Martha's Vineyard with her family. Maggie and John were with Christian and the Diadores, and Sabrina joined Devon, Sascha, and Danielle for in-town shopping and a tour of the lighthouse.

The day flew by with shopping and relaxing and zero expectations from Sascha, and she loved it. While the Montagues and Sabrina walked the beaches and toured the lighthouse, the bride-to-be spent the day with her bridesmaids getting plucked, waxed, and a spray tan so dark that her skin was darker than Sascha's caramel complexion.

By the time the rehearsal dinner arrived, Sascha was feeling blissful. Spending the day with her loved ones, soaking up the sun, had filled Sascha with joy, and her serotonin levels were overflowing. She and Devon entered the rehearsal dinner holding hands, madly in love, and smiling at each other. The couple found their assigned seats and were seated with Sascha's father, John, Maggie, and Sabrina.

"I love seeing you two so happy and in love," Maggie said as her eyes welled up with tears.

John rubbed Maggie's back to comfort her, and Sascha realized Maggie was sad for her son. Christian would not have the marriage that Devon and Sascha had for many reasons, and while that also made Sascha sad as well, she could tell it was breaking his mother's heart. Sascha reached out and took Maggie's hand in hers just as the couple was making their entrance. There was no denying they made a striking pair, but there was something ominous about the mood in the room that evening.

As the night went on with speeches and toasts, Sascha indulged in the Mediterranean feast served for dinner. She was in gyro heaven and gave herself permission to try a little bit of everything. Sascha sat back in her seat, unable to eat another bite, and people watched everyone at the gathering. The dynamic between Yvonne and her sisters and their mom was fascinating. They seemed to truly dislike her. While family drama played out, Christian seemed oblivious, even jovial in spite of everything. Sascha was not sure what to think about anything she was witnessing, but from the smirk on Sabrina's face, she was not the only one noticing.

About an hour later, Devon and Sascha took the path back to their cottage. It was a warm night with a full moon and the perfect setting for a romantic walk with her gallant husband. Fingers intertwined, the couple walked and talked about the delicious food served at the dinner, politics and Christian's upcoming election, and how her latest book was going. They were both careful to avoid any mention of Michael, but he was there, like always, in the back of their minds.

Arriving at the cottage, they found their usual golf cart driver waiting. They sent Lena back to the main house with the driver and got ready for bed. Danielle was asleep, and although it was late, Sascha was not ready for sleep just yet.

"Ugh, so much yummy bread and pasta. Not sure I'll fit into my dress tomorrow," Sascha said as she undressed.

"Your dress will fit fine, and you will look perfect," Devon said as he stopped undressing to look at his tall, fit wife standing in her underwear.

"Well, I was thinking, just to be on the safe side, I needed to burn off some extra calories tonight," Sascha stated, removing her bra.

Devon came and stood in front of Sascha, cupping her full breasts as he used his thumbs to tease her nipples. "Would this help?" he whispered, bending down to kiss the base of her neck.

"Oh yes, Mr. Montague. I think you are on to something," Sascha said with a throaty laugh as Devon tossed her onto the bed.

Sascha fell asleep two hours later, spent and with a smile on her face.

Sascha awoke the next morning to birds chirping and the sun shining through a cottage window. Standing up to stretch her achy back, she heard Sabrina's voice coming from the main living area. Putting on a robe, Sascha went out to greet her sister.

"Morning, Brina. What are you doing here so early?"

"Early? It's nearly 8:00 a.m., and we were supposed to

meet this morning for yoga and meditation," Sabrina said, eyeing her sister. "But it looks like you may have had a late night."

"Would you settle for a nice walk this morning?" Sascha asked with a quick look to her husband who winked at her.

Sabrina chuckled, looking from her sister to her brother-in-law. "A walk it is. I'm going to be outside stretching while you get ready. Do you want to come stretch with auntie?" Sabrina asked, turning to Danielle, who eagerly agreed.

Sascha planted a long, lingering kiss on her husband's lips before hurrying off to get dressed.

SASCHA, Devon, and Danielle walked the path from their cottage to the location of the wedding. It was a beautiful day for the wedding. The sun was shining bright, not a cloud in the sky, and there was a light breeze that made the temperature perfect. Sascha caught the smell of hyacinths and jasmine in the air and realized there were hundreds of flowers hanging everywhere.

Sascha dressed in a simple blue, tea-length dress with a scoop neckline and short sleeves, which paired nicely with Devon who was dressed in a dark-blue suit, crisp white shirt, and a blue-striped tie. They made a striking couple, and as they passed other wedding guests on their way to their destination, they turned heads. They each held Danielle's hand as she skipped and requested to be swung between them. Their little Danielle wore a crepe blue-and-white flower-patterned dress, white tights, and black Mary Jane shoes. She was a beautiful little girl, who had her mother's soft, golden-brown curls and her father's green eyes.

It was an outdoor wedding set against the backdrop of the Atlantic Ocean. When Sascha and Devon walked up to the wedding site, the two hundred–plus guests were being seated as a string quartet played music. The chairs and the aisle were all accented with flowers and greenery, while the altar was completely covered in flowers. The white and gold decor was complemented by dark blues and purple flowers as the fragrance permeated the salty air.

The Montagues took their seats on the groom's side just as Christian was walking up to the altar. Sascha waved and greeted Sabrina, her father, and Maggie, who were already seated, and then turned her focus to Christian. He looked handsome, Sascha noted, but also like he was going to vomit at any minute. He searched the crowd, and his eyes found Sascha's. His eyes pleaded with her, for what she was not sure, but she mouthed the words, *It will be all right.* Christian nodded his head in response, took a deep breath, and appeared to be calmer.

Sascha felt terrible for Christian. He did not want to marry Yvonne, but he did want to settle down, he wanted a family, and he wanted to be a congressman. Marrying Yvonne helped him achieve all of those goals, but at what cost? Christian was choosing to settle for Yvonne because he could not have who he wanted—her—and Sascha knew all too well that marriages built on settling or pleasing others instead of for love and friendship were destined for unhappiness and failure.

The quartet's music began playing louder as the bridesmaids and groomsmen came down the aisle. The groomsmen, one of whom was Yvonne's awful brother, all wore the traditional black tuxedo, while all the bridesmaids wore strapless champagne-colored dresses that hugged their figures. And of course they all had amazing figures. Yvonne would never allow a less-than-perfect bridesmaid into her wedding party. Sascha also noticed that neither of her sisters were bridesmaids.

The wedding march started as a stunning Yvonne came down the aisle on the arm of her father. Yvonne wore a designer strapless wedding gown, which complemented her tall, thin figure. The wedding dress bodice was corseted and showed off her enviable tiny waist. Yvonne wore her straight brown hair in a half-up, half-down do with a delicate silk veil covering her face. Arriving at the altar, Christian lifted her veil, and Sascha saw the excited, joyous expression on Yvonne's face, which was in stark contrast to the serious, focused expression on Christian's. The wedding ceremony was over quickly as the bride and groom exchanged vows, rings, and what appeared to be a chaste kiss. It was painful to watch for Sascha, but she hoped the other guests did not pick up on the groom's reluctance.

After the ceremony concluded, the bride and groom went off for wedding pictures, while Sascha and Devon walked Danielle back to their cottage where Lena awaited them to put Danielle down for her nap. Sascha chatted with Lena briefly about how things were going for her at the big house in the "servants'" quarters, and while she laughed at the ridiculous, distinct separation between the "help" and the family and guests, she said she was enjoying the location and had met some great people.

Once Danielle fell asleep, Sascha and Devon returned to the wedding reception and left Danielle in Lena's care, with instructions to notify them once she was up from her nap. Arriving at the wedding reception venue, gone was the string quartet, and in their place was a DJ, playing a good mix of music genres. Sascha bopped to an eighties tune as she filled two small plates with fruit and cheeses, while Devon went to grab them drinks. She was starving.

After filling the plates, Sascha went in search of their assigned seats. Finding their table, which was right in front of the wedding party's location, Sascha quickly sat down as she was starting to feel tired.

The festivities began shortly after Sascha took her seat with the bride and groom being introduced. Sascha recognized they made a stunning pair as she looked on while they took their first dance as a married couple. Yvonne had changed into another designer dress and changed her hairstyle as well to let all of her hair down with a beach-wave effect to her shoulder-length hair. As the couple danced to a classic love song, talking about staying together forever, Sascha could not help but see the irony in the words.

Sascha found watching Christian's and Yvonne's display of false happiness depressing and decided to focus on the delicious food spread in front of her instead. The dinner consisted of lobster bisque, shrimp scampi, and the choice of either surf and turf or a pasta dish for the main course. Sascha was ravenous and nibbled off both her and Devon's plates. As he chuckled at his wife's increased appetite, Sascha received a text from Lena that Danielle was awake and up.

"Our girl is up. I'm going to go get her," Sascha said, starting to stand up.

"Absolutely not, love," Devon said, putting his hand on his wife's back. "Please sit down and relax, and I'll go grab her and be back shortly."

AFTER THE BRIDE and groom shared their first dance, many of the wedding guests hit the dance floor. Sascha watched her sister and father on the dance floor, dancing to one of her late mother's favorite songs. Sascha's eyes filled with tears, but she could not help but smile at the sight of them laughing and honoring her mom in a small way.

Sascha and Devon danced a few times, and that was enough for her. She was tired. Sascha, Devon, and Danielle were sitting, enjoying scrumptious wedding cake, when Francesca, Yvonne's sister, came over with her young son and sat with them. As Devon conversed with an old college friend who was also in attendance at the wedding, Francesca chatted Sascha up.

"I have to ask," Francesca said with a curious expression on her face. "After the situation with Michael Ghant, does it not bother you that he and Yvonne used to date?"

Sascha's heart stopped, and she held her breath for a moment at Francesca's words. *Surely this woman knows I am not aware of Michael's association with Yvonne*, Sascha thought. Regardless of whether there was no malicious intent or if Francesca was being vindictive toward her sister, Sascha refused to give her the reaction she was hoping for.

With a smile on her face, Sascha stated, "It does not matter to me. Michael is irrelevant in my life."

Francesca appeared to be disappointed with Sascha's response and quickly made an excuse to leave and go stir the pot elsewhere.

Meanwhile Sascha was shocked and furious. How did she not know about this? So many secrets and lies with so many people in her life. Not able to sit any longer and pretend she was not fuming, Sascha told Devon she was ready to call it a night. They rode back silently in the golf cart as Devon held their sleeping daughter. Once Sascha got Danielle into her pajamas and tucked in for the night, Sascha went back out to the living area.

"Did you know that Michael and Yvonne used to date?"

"Seriously? When?"

"I guess right before he and Cate got together," Sascha said incredulously.

"Wow, so the plot thickens," Devon said, shaking his head. "Wait, so is that what her sister was up to tonight sitting with you?"

"Yep!"

"What a weird family," Devon said as he pulled Sascha into his arms.

"Yes, they are weirdos, and I guess it does not really matter at this point, but I think Yvonne should have told me about her past with Michael."

"Do you think Christian knows?" Devon asked.

"Knows that he married a woman who previously dated the person who was coconspirators with the woman who killed his beloved big brother? I don't think so."

"He has to be told."

"Yes, but just not on his wedding night."

CHAPTER 13

*E*lection Day had finally arrived, and Sascha was so excited for Christian's big event. In college she had volunteered on multiple campaigns and used to be much more active in politics than she was now. She realized she had missed the action a little bit. There was something addictive and electric about politics and the power.

Sascha and Sabrina had been working the phones at Christian's Illinois election headquarters for days leading up to Election Day. Sascha and Devon also made multiple appearances with Christian at rallies and gave their public endorsement for the young politician. Sascha used her celebrity status to promote Christian on social media, but the help did not appear to be needed since he had a huge following of women in love with his boyish good looks and charm. Add to that the fact that he had just married Yvonne Diadore, whose family was practically considered American royalty, he was sure to win. It was a fairy tale, at least that was how several news outlets had referred to Christian and Yvonne's romance and relationship, but like all fairy tales, theirs was full of loss, deception, and lies.

"What are you thinking about?" Christian asked quietly, walking up behind Sascha and startling her. Turning around, Sascha gave her stepbrother a soft smile, and he returned that smile with a look of pure love and adoration.

"I was just thinking how proud I am of you and that I think you are actually going to do this. I think you are going to win."

"It means a lot to me that you are here," Christian said in a lowered voice as he held Sascha's gaze and took a step toward her.

"We're both super excited to be here to support you, brother!" Sabrina proclaimed as she walked up and gave Christian a hug from the side.

Christian's face flushed as he broke his gaze with Sascha, gave a nod to the women, and walked away.

"Oh my god, Brina, I have no idea where that was going, but I'm pretty sure you just saved me."

"Oh, I know, and you're welcome." Sabrina giggled as she walked back to her station.

The rest of the day flew by in a blur. By the time the polls closed, Sascha was exhausted and ready to go to bed. Devon had headed back to the hotel to read Danielle a bedtime story and put her to sleep, and Sascha was incredibly envious. The rest of the family all gathered at a suite at the campaign headquarters as poll numbers started coming in. Christian was off to a quick lead, but a lot of votes were still left to be counted, and it was expected to be a long night.

Sascha looked around the room, and the tension was palpable. Multiple televisions were on, all on different news channels, watching the election results come in. Sabrina sat on a couch watching mindless videos on social media, while Maggie crocheted, and Sascha's dad played a game of solitaire.

As Sascha sat in an armchair with a cup of coffee, Christian paced the room, reminding Sascha of his big brother, Colin. Christian had a serious expression on his face, but Sascha knew deep inside he was a nervous wreck. Sascha understood his nervousness, but his pacing was making her anxious. Making eye contact with Yvonne who was stiffly sitting watching the news, Sascha motioned for her to go over and comfort and calm her man down, but she shook her head, declining to deal with her husband.

Deciding to take pity on her stepbrother, Sascha went over to Christian and asked him to take a walk with her. He stopped pacing and stared at her in surprise, then nodded his head and followed her out of the room. As they walked out of the room, Maggie briefly stopped crocheting, and Yvonne crossed her arms and glared furiously at the pair.

Once out in the hall, Christian asked, "Where are we going?"

"To a really nice spot I found earlier. Come on," Sascha said as they got into the elevator.

Exiting the elevator at a rooftop bar, Sascha motioned for Christian to continue to follow her. Sascha led him through the bar and out to a large balcony. Stepping outside, the cool, crisp air was like a splash of cold water.

As they leaned against the railing, staring up at the stars, Sascha asked, "Are you scared?"

"Yeah," he whispered.

"Of losing or winning?"

Christian continued to stare up at the night sky for a few moments before answering.

"Both."

"I know it's scary. You want something so bad, but then you also have fears about getting what you want most. You ask yourself, what if it's not what I thought it would be? What if I am not good enough?"

"Are you talking about writing, politics, or us?" Christian asked, turning to face Sascha.

"Christian, there is no us, at least not like that, but yes, it does apply to my writing career and your political career. Failure is scary and so is success, but I think you can handle either. We both can."

Christian smiled slightly and started to speak when both their phones chimed. Checking her phone, Sascha saw they were about to make an election call in Christian's congressional race. They hurried back down to the suite, and before entering Christian said, "You give great advice. Would it be okay to just call sometimes when I need someone to talk to and to talk some sense into me?"

"Of course, we are family. So long as the calls are not of a romantic nature, we are good."

Christian stared into Sascha's eyes one last time before they entered the room just in time to hear him announced as the winner of his congressional district. Christian's campaign manager grabbed Christian and congratulated him, and they quickly began preparation for his victory speech, which would take place in fifteen minutes in a large conference room downstairs filled with his campaign volunteers and supporters.

Sascha stood off to the side as Christian and Yvonne took to the stage to address his supporters. Sascha smiled in pride, and Maggie walked up beside her and took her hand. Christian was an inspirational speaker and a force to be reckoned with.

"Thank you for being the big sister and friend he needed today," Maggie said as she wiped away tears. Sascha leaned over and hugged Maggie.

"Like I told him, we're family."

As Christian wrapped up his speech, the room started

chanting his name. There were high hopes for him, and Sascha could see his bright future.

"That man is going to be president one day" was the statement said by multiple people in the room, and Sascha could not disagree.

Pulling out her phone from her small handbag to take pictures, Sascha saw multiple missed messages. Clicking on one message from an unknown number, Sascha saw she had been sent a photo with a caption that said, "I'm jealous." It was a photo of her and Christian from the rooftop. A snapshot of a moment in time, but the photo appeared intimate as Christian's feelings for her were on full display.

Michael! Sascha thought as she closed her phone and began looking around the crowd. There was no way he was out there, but one of his minions was. Feeling herself become light-headed, Sascha took a deep breath and thought, *Not tonight.* Refusing to let Michael ruin another event, Sascha pushed the horrible thoughts to the back of her mind and plastered a fake smile on her face.

CHAPTER 14

Sascha was tired but still exhilarated from the previous night's event at Christian's election head-quarters. Michael had tried to ruin the night with his little photo stunt, but last night she was able to block him out of her mind and focus on her family. The look on Maggie's face when it was announced that her son had been elected to the United States Congress was priceless. She was so proud of him, but Sascha could tell she was also sad to not have Colin there to celebrate with her and his little brother. Sascha caught Maggie's gaze as she hugged her son, and Sascha nodded slightly to her as she knew they both were thinking the same thing.

Now that Christian and Yvonne were married and his election was over, Sascha longed for life to settle down for everyone and return to normalcy. Well, at least as normal as it could be with her stalker, Michael, still on the loose. She hoped the newlyweds found happiness together but doubted the possibility. While Sascha did not care for Yvonne, Yvonne seemed to be very much in love with Christian, which was the most important thing as far as Sascha was concerned. Yvonne's feelings for Sascha were mutual, but Sascha would do everything in her power to get along with Yvonne and assure her that nothing would ever happen between her and Christian. Clearing her mind of family drama, Sascha focused on her first love.

Sascha was back to her writing routine and had spent the last week writing for nearly ten hours straight daily. As she stood at the stove cooking dinner, Sascha rubbed her achy back, which had started to hurt from so much sitting during her long days of writing. As if on cue, Sascha felt strong hands against her back, rubbing her sore muscles.

"Here, let me help you," Devon said as he wrapped his arms around Sascha and pulled her into his arms and kissed her neck.

"Umm, Mr. Montague, how is this helping my sore back?" Sascha giggled as her husband kissed and nipped at her neck.

"Is this not helping?" he continued, turning her around to face him. Sascha stared into her charming husband's eyes and felt flutters in her stomach. "How it is that you are getting more beautiful and sexier by the day?" Devon murmured in her ear.

Devon pulled Sascha into a passionate kiss and away from the stove. "I want you, now," Devon demanded, and Sascha was eager to oblige until she smelled something burning on the stove.

Pulling away, Sascha teased, "Sorry, love, it will need to wait until after dinner."

"I can wait. I just don't want to," he responded with a boyish grin.

Sascha giggled as she looked down and noticed an incoming call from her dad on her watch. She searched the room with her eyes, looking for her phone to take the call, but it was nowhere to be found. Thinking she likely left it in her home office, Sascha asked Devon to keep an eye on dinner while she went to go find her phone.

As Sascha opened her office door, she was startled to find Delilah in there, and with Sascha's phone in her hand.

"What are you doing in here?" Sascha demanded as she watched her phone fall from Delilah hands.

"I...I...was walking by the room and heard your phone ringing and thought to grab it and bring it to you." Delilah seemed nervous at first but then recovered and responded in her usual arrogant manner.

"And you closed the door behind you?"

"I have no idea how that happened," Delilah replied, and she bent down to recover Sascha's phone.

Sascha did not believe a word coming out of the woman's mouth, but she now knew for certain she was up to no good, and her scheme was not just about Devon.

"I'll take that," Sascha said, sticking out her hand, waiting for Delilah to hand over her phone to her.

"My office is off-limits to everyone except Devon and Tatum."

"Understood," Delilah calmly stated, but Sascha could tell she was flustered and angry.

Waving her hand toward the door, Sascha glared at Delilah until she left the room.

When Sascha returned to the kitchen, Devon was telling Delilah to have a nice evening as he was grabbing plates for their dinner.

"Did you find your phone?" Devon asked, before turning around to see his wife's heated face. "What's wrong? Is it bad news from your dad?"

"Oh, that's right. I almost forgot. Let me give my dad a call back," Sascha stated as she dialed her father.

"Hi, Dad, sorry I missed your call."

As Sascha spoke on the phone with her father, she began biting her lip as she felt her anxiety climb. Devon put his hand on Sascha's back and rubbed it in a soothing motion. Knowing his wife, he seemed to recognize an anxiety attack was coming on. Hanging up with her father, she put her hand to her chest, closed her eyes, and breathed deeply as she worked to calm herself.

"What's happened?" Devon asked, after Sascha took a few moments to gather herself.

"My dad interrupted a break-in and was assaulted," Sascha stated with an incredulous expression.

"What? Is he all right?"

"Yes, it sounds like it. He says he was hit over the head with something and was found unconscious by Maggie."

"Who would do this?" Devon asked with suspicion in his eyes.

"I have no idea. Christian was just elected, so I suppose it could be related to that, but I doubt it. I would think that if it were related to Christian's election, then the break-in would have been before Election Day not after," Sascha said as she hunched her shoulders in confusion.

"Well, if the break-in was not about Christian, it was about you."

"Michael?"

"Yes. He could be showing us that he still has a long reach and can get to your loved ones if he wants to."

"Or it could have been a random break-in, which does happen," Sascha responded, not wanting to think about Michael at the moment.

Devon stared at his wife without comment for a few moments before he pulled Sascha into an embrace, kissed the top of her head, and said, "I'll make some calls and have it checked into."

Sascha leaned her head into her husband's chest and whispered, "Let's eat. I'm starving." But she found she had little appetite once they sat down to eat.

CHAPTER 15

Sascha woke up early and achy the next morning. Experiencing pain, she decided to forgo the treadmill and her usual run and instead replace her normal exercise routine with stretching and yoga. Her back still hurt and now so did the rest of her body as Devon had made love to her several times that night. He took her in the library after dinner, then in the shower later that evening, and again in the middle of the night. Sascha smiled to herself. What had come over her husband, Sascha did not know, but she hoped too much of a good thing would never be the case with their sex life.

Looking over at her sleeping husband, Sascha could not help but reach out and gently caress her love. Devon stirred slightly at her touch but did not wake up. Sascha was certain he was just as tired as she was. *He put in a lot of work last night,* she thought, and giggled to herself as she walked into her closet to get ready.

Sascha dressed in yoga pants and a sweatshirt before heading downstairs to get her day started. After putting on a pot of coffee, she went into her gym, did some stretches, and then streamed a yoga class. Feeling less achy and more ready for the day ahead, Sascha walked back into the kitchen to pour herself a cup of coffee. It was a chilly morning, so Sascha decided to take her coffee in the library next to the fireplace. As she sat sipping from her large mug and watching the news, she heard sirens.

At first she thought nothing of the noise. It was not completely unusual to hear the occasional ambulance siren in the Swell as there were quite a few elderly neighbors in the community, but on this day, the amount of sirens Sascha heard go by outside caused her to get up from her chair and walk outside to see what was going on.

Quickly putting on her sneakers, Sascha went for the front door and found Matt going in the same direction.

"Do you know why there are so many sirens?"

"No, but I heard at least four police cars go by," Matt stated as he opened the front door for Sascha and then followed her out to the front of the home.

As they approached the road, Sascha noticed many other neighbors standing outside their homes as well and spotted Anna approaching her from across the street.

"Good morning, Anna, do you know what's going on?" Sascha asked, and she saw a van marked Forensics drive past.

"Well, some people are saying a body has been found," Anna whispered.

"What? A body? Whose body?" Sascha rapidly fired off questions.

Matt told Sascha he was going to find out what was going on and started in the direction the sirens had gone.

"Matt, take one of the golf carts. It will be faster," Sascha said, and Matt made a beeline for the two parked golf carts outside their garage area.

Seeing Matt take off in the direction of the woods at the Swell, Sascha turned her attention back to Anna.

"I only know about the body because some of the neighbors are saying the Knapps were out jogging this morning and found a body in the woods," Anna stated, while her eyes followed Matt as he drove down the street. "Oh my god, that man is so hot. Tell Sabrina if she doesn't want him, I will take him."

"Really, Anna! You're talking about this right now?" Sascha scolded her friend.

"Sorry, I have been really horny lately, and besides, we don't even know if there really is a body out there, right?"

"Hopefully there is not one, but after seeing a forensics van go by, I'm thinking that's probably a bad sign." Sascha continued looking down the street for a few moments before shaking her head, deciding to let the matter drop for now. "Come on in and join me for a cup of coffee. Matt will find out what's going on."

Entering the house, Sascha found her husband coming toward her.

"Morning, Anna," Devon said as he nodded to Anna before turning to greet his wife with a soft kiss. "Did I hear a bunch of sirens earlier?"

"Yes, you did. Allegedly a body has been found in the woods," Sascha responded as she took her husband by the hand and ushered him and Anna into the kitchen.

"A human body? Here?" Devon said with surprise in his voice.

"Excuse me, ma'am, where did you want to take breakfast this morning?" asked Corrine, one of the Montagues' housekeepers. Corrine held a large platter with fresh fruit, pastries, and a generous bowl of oatmeal.

"Good morning, Corrine. The breakfast room, please. Thank you," Sascha said as the group followed Corrine. "Hey, Corrine, do you by any chance know what's going on out there in the woods?" Sascha knew that if anyone knew what was going on it would be one of the house staff members. It was a poorly kept secret that the house employees had their own network of gossip and community intel.

Corrine set the platter on the table and turned to face the group. As all eyes in the room focused on Corrine, she started to get fidgety.

"Corrine, it's all right. Whatever you tell us will stay within this room," Sascha softly stated.

Corrine's eyes briefly darted to Anna before she nodded her head and said, "A woman's body has been found in the woods. No one is exactly sure who it is, but rumors are that it is one of the women from the Bougie Mafia."

Both Sascha and Anna gasped in shock at Corinne's revelation.

"The Bougie Mafia? What the hell is that?" Devon asked with a confused look on his face.

"Thank you, Corinne," Sascha said, dismissing the woman before turning to her husband to offer an explanation.

Sascha shook her head, embarrassed that she even knew who the Bougie Mafia were but explained it to her husband.

"Wow, okay, so I really have no idea about what's going on in this community, but if what we're hearing is true, I'm very sorry for whomever that is out there, but I am so glad that we do not associate with these people," Devon said, and he popped a blueberry into his mouth.

"Well, this is terrible for the family of whoever it is. Kerri and Lucy are moms with young children," Anna stated.

"What about the Marissa woman?"

"Marissa had what she deserved, no one, except for a rich, old husband who did not want to be bothered with her. Rumor has it that he is divorcing her," Anna stated with venom in her voice.

"Ouch, that's pretty harsh, Anna," Sascha said as Devon gave her a pointed look.

"It is, and I feel terrible for saying this, but I hate her. A lot of people do. And you probably would too if she were sleeping with your husband," Anna said with irritation in her voice.

Sascha quietly nodded her head. Sascha understood Anna's anger toward Marissa; she, too, had been there before, with her ex-husband and his cheating, but before she could say this to Anna, Matt walked into the room.

"Matt, did you find out anything?"

Matt nodded his head with a serious expression on his face.

"Well, who is it?" Sascha demanded, not wanting to wait any longer.

"The body found was Marissa Tanner."

Sascha was speechless. While they had been speculating that morning, nothing felt real until that moment.

"How did she die? Was it a possible suicide?" Devon asked.

"No. It was murder. A brutal murder," Matt said, and the room went eerily silent.

CHAPTER 16

News of Marissa Tanner's murder rippled through the Swell and the entire country's high society. All major news outlets were covering the story, and it was nearly impossible to get in and out of the gates of the Swell as the streets were filled with camera crews, reporters, and spectators, which forced many of the residents to use a secret, gated backroad that led in and out of the forest.

The brutal murder of anyone is always a terrifying and salacious news story, but for a murder of this nature to occur in the exclusive, gated community of the Swell was unheard of. The police were leaving no stone unturned in their investigation, and the suspect list was long. Marissa had made a lot of enemies and had a lot of dirt on many powerful people. But was one of those powerful individuals willing to kill her to keep her quiet? And even if they were willing to kill her, would they do it themselves rather than hire a professional killer? It seemed like an impossible murder to solve.

Sascha loved a good mystery and a challenge and believed solving Marissa's murder would be both. Sascha had started to make her own list of possible suspects in Marissa's death.

The obvious suspect was her husband, but he was elderly and primarily resided out of state. Also, he was divorcing her with an iron-clad prenuptial agreement in place, which made his motivation and opportunity pretty low in Sascha's mind. In Sascha's opinion the police needed to be checking into the alibis for the many pissed-off wives whose husbands were sleeping with Marissa, or the husbands themselves who were rich and powerful men who did not want a soon-to-be single Marissa tarnishing their good name and reputation.

Sascha hated to admit it, but while Marissa Tanner's murder was a horrible tragedy, it was also an intriguing distraction from her own life's stresses. Thinking about Marissa and playing whodunit meant Sascha was not thinking about Michael and where he could be and what he was plotting next. And there was no doubt in her mind that Michael was plotting. With her hand-to-hand combat and weapons training, Sascha had no qualms about her ability to best Michael in a fair fight, but Michael did not believe in fighting fair. Michael's modus operandi was to isolate, disorient, and incapacitate with a stun gun and then repro-gram and control with a syringe full of ketamine. He was methodical, he was disciplined, and worst of all, he was patient.

As Sascha sat with her thoughts of Michael and her list of possible suspects, her doorbell rang. She had been expecting the police. They were questioning everyone who lived and worked in the Swell, including all house staff. She was not sure what to expect but felt prepared since she always watched true crime television and procedural dramas.

Sascha answered her door and found two detectives standing there, and they were an interesting pair. A dark-skinned, petite, older woman with slightly graying hair and a large man with white-blond hair and hands the size of catcher's gloves greeted Sascha. *Hmm,* she thought as she got the feeling this interview would be nothing like television.

They introduced themselves as Detective Davis and Detective Lund, informed her they were questioning all the neighbors about Marissa's murder, and asked where they could conduct the meetings. Sascha showed them to her great room, where they would individually interview her, Devon, and all their staff. They followed Sascha's lead, and as they walked, they looked around the large home, especially Detective Davis, seemingly making mental notes and searching for possible clues. Sascha could not tell from the looks on their faces if they were impressed, envious, or judging her grand lifestyle.

After offering them drinks, which they both declined, Sascha settled herself on a comfortable suede couch with a cup of coffee in hand and waited for them to be seated as well in the club chairs across from her. She studied them as they made awkward eye contact with one another. *Hmm, they must be new partners,* Sascha thought. She could tell they did not know each other well and had not found their rhythm yet as they both started asking her questions at the same time.

Detective Lund nodded his head at Detective Davis and allowed her to take the lead. Without hesitation, Detective Davis started in with questions, and they were all questions Sascha had anticipated. Sascha watched and read a lot of true crime, but being the one in the hot seat being questioned was nerve-racking. She felt nervous even though she had nothing to hide.

After gathering her thoughts and calming her nerves, Sascha felt ready to respond. Sascha stated she did not know Marissa very well and had only interacted with her a few times. She had never socialized with her outside of neighborhood events, but she had seen her once or twice at restaurants, the theater, and charity events.

"And who was she usually with at these events?" Detective Davis asked as she looked up from her notepad.

"No idea. I noticed her but didn't pay much attention past that."

"Did Marissa have any enemies?"

The question gave Sascha a hearty laugh, and her laughter was met with a confused look from Detective Lund and a harsh glare from Detective Davis.

"Do you find the brutal murder of a young woman funny, Mrs. Montague?" Detective Davis glared at her with dark eyes as she scolded her.

"Of course not, and I shouldn't have laughed. It's just that Marissa pissed off a lot of people, and she was known to be quite the mean girl. Plus she also had a fondness for married men. Very powerful and wealthy married men. So yeah, she had a lot of enemies, and the list of her enemies is long," Sascha stated, still feeling guilty for laughing.

With a quick glance at each other, the detectives stated they were done with their questions for her and asked to speak with Matt.

"Okay, but why specifically Matt? He is my private security guard and a good guy."

"Ma'am, we're just following up on some information we received," Detective Davis responded, attempting to dismiss Sascha. But Sascha would not be dismissed so easily, and she was protective of her staff.

"Look, I'm sure it would be so much easier for everyone if the killer were my butler or footman, but it's more likely she was killed by a peer. I mean, look at where she was found. She was clearly out there meeting someone."

"You have a real-life butler and footman?" Detective Lund excitedly asked.

Sascha peered at the man in frustration. "No, that was sarcasm. I will go get Matt for you." Sascha walked away and shook her head, wondering if the killer would ever be caught with someone like Detective Lund working the case. Or perhaps that was the purpose of assigning him to it. Sascha made a mental note to look into city officials who may have been involved with Marissa.

The detectives spent a couple of hours more at the Montague residence interviewing the staff. Sascha was relieved when they finally left, but they promised to be in touch—whatever that meant. Despite her earlier laugh, Sascha was uncomfortable with the thought that there was likely still a murderer in the neighborhood. She doubted the culprit lived outside the gates of the Swell, and at the very least, the killer had access to the Swell. Sascha also felt certain the one who held the knife over Marissa's body and took her life was privileged and had their expensive defense attorney on standby.

Closing the door behind the detectives, Sascha went to locate Devon to find out what questions he was asked. She found Devon and Matt together in his office discussing their interviews.

"Seriously? You two are in here commiserating over your interviews and no one bothered to come get me?" Sascha chided as she entered the office.

"Actually, we were discussing you," Devon said as his chiseled face focused on her.

"Me? Why me?" Sascha asked, confused by the statement.

"I should be leaving," Matt said, turning to leave the room.

"Ah, Matt, not so fast," Sascha said in a tone that was not a suggestion.

Devon chuckled and walked around from behind his desk to stand by his wife.

"Your safety is both mine and Matt's number one concern. And with this Marissa woman's murder, we will need to be extra careful until her killer is caught. Even the Swell is not safe right now," Devon said softly as he brushed back a curl from her face.

"Has it ever been safe for me here?" Sascha asked, and she recalled the night Michael attacked her in their home.

"This is different, Sascha, and you know it," Devon responded, observing his wife with suspicion, while Matt shifted uncomfortably by the door.

"I agree. Both were targeted attacks. Mine was by Michael, and Marissa's was by some enemy of hers," Sascha responded defiantly.

"That will be all, Matt," Devon said, and Matt quickly exited the room, closing the door behind him.

Devon stared at Sascha quietly with soft eyes while she returned his gaze with stubbornness.

"Sweetheart, I do not want you getting involved in whatever is going on here. It's not safe, and I want you far away from any more danger. Don't we already have our hands full with Michael?"

"Yep, we sure do," Sascha said to her husband.

"Good, then it's agreed?" Devon asked as he looked at Sascha expectantly.

Sascha nodded and left his office while thinking, *Fine, I'll deal with Michael first, but then I'll find Marissa Tanner's killer.*

CHAPTER 17

Sascha walked into her favorite restaurant, Gabriel's at Fisherman's Wharf, with a big smile on her face, excited to be meeting up with her sister and Cate for drinks. It had been a while since they had all been out together, and she really missed spending time with them. The first to arrive, Sascha was quickly seated and happily waited for the women to join her. In the meantime Sascha ordered a round of drinks for everyone and enjoyed the view of boats coming in and out of the San Francisco harbor.

Cate arrived just as the waiter was setting down their drinks, and she looked fantastic. You would never have known it by looking at her, but a year ago she had nearly died at the hands of her husband and Sascha's friend turned enemy Michael Ghant. Early on in their marriage, Michael began isolating Cate and drugging her to manipulate and control her. Cate slowly became a shell of the woman she once was and started withdrawing from her friendship with Sascha. At first Sascha thought Cate's changes in behavior were due to jealousy of her friendship with Michael and Michael's romantic feelings for Sascha, which would be troubling for any wife. Shockingly the truth behind the changes in Cate and what was actually happening in the Ghant household was like something out of a horror movie.

Although Cate had been pushing Sascha away, Sascha was determined to figure out what was going on with her best friend, and she desperately wanted to mend their friendship. Sascha eventually learned that while Cate was drugged, Michael began planting negative thoughts in Cate's head in an attempt to gaslight her and make her go crazy and hopefully kill herself. It nearly worked, but with the help of Sabrina, Sascha was able to get Cate out of Michael's clutches and into a facility to help her detox and recover from the mental and emotional abuse she had endured. In the facility Cate slowly recovered memories and returned to her old self, and when she did, she saw red and wanted to kill Michael. Unfortunately Michael nearly killed Cate instead, leaving her for dead, shot and floating facedown in their home pool. Once again Sascha and Sabrina came to the rescue, but Michael was nowhere to be found until he showed up at Sascha's home with the intention of kidnapping her.

"You're looking beautiful as always but also super fit. Your body looks insane. What are you doing different?" Cate asked as she pulled back from their hug and admired Sascha's figure.

"Thank you," Sascha responded as she blushed. "Well, I am still running nearly every day, but I think the big physical changes are coming from Krav Maga. Matt and I have started weapons training, and I'm not gonna lie, I feel like a total badass."

"Well, you look like a badass to me," Cate responded, and her big blue eyes shimmered in the light as she sat and sipped the drink Sascha had ordered.

Sabrina arrived a few moments later with flushed cheeks.

Both women looked at her with questions in their eyes, but she said, "Don't ask. It has been a day."

Grabbing the margarita Sascha had waiting on the table for her, Sabrina took a few sips before diving into chat with the ladies.

"Okay, what did I miss?" Sabrina asked excitedly.

"Nothing really, Cate just got here."

"Great because I want all the juicy details about the murder at the Swell," Sabrina requested, and then both her and Cate cast their eager eyes onto Sascha.

"Yes, I want to hear all about the murder, and then I have a different topic I want to discuss," Cate chimed in.

"Well, honestly, I don't know much," Sascha said.

"That's fine. Tells us what you do know," Sabrina prompted.

"All right. So as you both probably already know, the victim was Marissa Tanner. She was found stabbed to death in the woods off one of the walking trails by a couple who lives in the Swell. And apparently it was pretty gruesome. There were a lot of stab wounds."

"Victim, huh? That woman had so many enemies because she was a horrible person. She had a lot of victims," Cate stated with disdain.

"So you knew her?" Sabrina asked Cate.

"We met a few times over the years, and I'm pretty sure she screwed Michael on multiple occasions."

"What? When?" Sascha asked, shocked.

"In my drug haze, I saw her leaving our home a few times last year. I would wake up and wander through the house sometimes in the middle of the night. Michael and I had stopped sharing a room, and half the time I had no idea if he was even home, but I saw her leaving in the early morning hours on more than one occasion with her hair disheveled, lipstick smudged, and barefoot. The crazy thing is that when she saw me, she gave me a haughty look that said, 'Yeah, I just screwed your man, and what are you going to do about it?' I was angry at the disrespect, but my brain would not allow me to react."

"Oh, Cate, I had no idea," Sascha said, putting her hand over Cate's.

"It's all right. Better than all right now, but I saw her for what she was, and so did Michael. She was looking for her next meal ticket, and if she had ended up with Michael, she would have deserved it," Cate said as she shook her head in disgust. Her beautiful auburn locks fell slightly into her face before she quickly brushed them away and continued. "Anyway, back to her murder. Who do we think most likely did it?"

"Well, isn't it always the husband?" Sabrina asked.

"Brina, I normally would think so too but not in this case. Her husband was divorcing her, and they had a prenup, and rumor has it that she was not going to get very much, which would explain why she was on the hunt for a new sugar daddy," Sascha said, looking to Cate. "Plus, they had no children, and he's an elderly man. I just don't see a legit motive on his part."

"Okay, all good points. So if not him, then who? I mean if there were a lot of stab wounds, I would say the murder was personal. Unless of course there is a serial killer on the loose, which would be really scary," Sabrina said.

"I think it was either one of the wives of her many lovers or one of her lovers who she was trying to shake down. My gut says it was a woman who killed her," Sascha responded, and she took a sip of her wine.

"Hmm, interesting," Cate said. "Wouldn't that make your friend Anna a suspect?"

"Technically yes, it would, but Anna would never do that. She and Tomas are divorced now, and he had many lovers.

Out of all the women he cheated with, why would she pick Marissa to murder?"

"I don't know, maybe opportunity," Cate suggested, and Sascha started to get defensive.

Before Sascha could respond, a waiter came to their table to take their orders. Sascha ordered her favorite Gabriel's specialty, although she did not have much of an appetite. Once the waiter left, Sascha immediately picked up where they left off.

"Tomas is not worth it, and Anna would never risk going to prison and being away from her girls just to kill a woman like Marissa."

"Never say never, Sascha. I'm sure two years ago you would have sworn Michael was a good man. People are very good at hiding their darkness."

Ouch, Sascha thought. Cate's words stung, but Sascha could not deny that she was right.

"I hear what you're saying, Cate," Sabrina chimed in. "But I just don't see Anna doing it either. I think it was probably someone else."

"I think so too, but for right now, in the Swell everyone is suspect. The police questioned me and my staff for hours the other day," Sascha admitted.

"Ooh, that sounds exciting."

"Not even close," Sascha said to her sister, giving her the side eye. "Trust me, it was not fun. And I don't think they have the best detectives on the case. One of them who interviewed me couldn't solve his way out of a paper bag, let alone solve a murder case."

"Wow! SFPD's finest, huh?" Sabrina said, and she laughed boisterously.

The women continued to speculate about the happenings at the Swell after their food arrived. Sascha was still not very hungry but had not eaten much today and knew she needed sustenance. Digging into her lobster mac and cheese, she appreciated the deliciousness of the food but felt queasy. Putting her fork down and picking up her glass of water, Sascha turned her attention back to their conversation.

"Anyway, Cate, what else did you want to talk about?" Sascha asked.

Finishing the bite of fish in her mouth, Cate took a sip from her wine glass and then stared pointedly at her friend.

"What the hell were you thinking hiring a woman like Delilah to be Devon's assistant?"

Sabrina's eyes got big at the question, but she said nothing at first. Sascha saw the expression on Sabrina's face as Cate asked the question and could tell her sister felt the same way.

"Listen, I trust Devon completely, and you know what I went through with Lucas, but truthfully, yes, I screwed up. If I had to do it all over again, I would have said I do not want to hire this person, but at the time I wanted to honor Emma's wishes and did not want to seem like an insecure, jealous wife."

"So fire her," Sabrina said firmly. "Devon would respect your wishes."

"Sascha, I agree, Devon is a good, trustworthy man, but, girl, you let a serpent into your house, and now you need to figure out how to get it out before it causes any damage. I watched her at the Orcas house, and she was definitely trying to get her claws into him. He seemed completely oblivious to it, but why tempt fate?" Cate said sternly.

Sascha still felt conflicted and had no idea what to do. Asking him to fire Delilah would sound like she was saying she did not trust Devon, which could not be further from the truth. Not wanting to discuss it any further, Sascha tried to change the topic, but Cate was not ready to drop it.

"Devon is crazy in love with you, almost to the point of

obsession, and I don't think he would ever stray, quite honestly, but something about that woman is off. She is completely untrustworthy and has an agenda. Just keep an eye on her," Cate said, and put her hands up, indicating she was done speaking her piece.

Sascha nodded as she took in the words and could not deny she felt the same way, but she would not dismiss Delilah until her motives were clear. Until that time Sascha would play the sweet, clueless wife and leave no evidence that she was onto Delilah's machinations.

The women talked more and ordered another round of drinks as they decided to plan a girls' weekend getaway to Sascha and Devon's newly renovated Montana ranch. While Sascha was an active participant in the planning and discussion for the trip, she could not stop thinking about the Delilah situation. She disliked Delilah, but she was truly angry with herself for not being honest with her husband. Sascha knew Sabrina and Cate were right. She just needed to figure out how to handle a snake without getting bit.

A couple of hours later, Sascha arrived home to find her husband sitting in the library, listening to music, and sipping a glass of wine. Kicking off her shoes, she sat down next to her husband and snuggled up to him.

"Were you waiting up for me?" Sascha asked, before planting a kiss on her husband's lips.

"Of course I was," he responded, and he cupped her face and pulled her back in for a more passionate kiss.

Pulling back, Sascha inquired about their daughter, whom Devon said was a perfect little angel for Dad while Mommy was away.

Sascha giggled as she felt her phone vibrate.

Who can that be? Sascha thought as she pulled out her phone and saw a message that made her speechless.

"What's going on?" Devon asked as Sascha handed him her phone.

The message was from Tomas Green, Anna's husband, and he said Anna was being arrested for Marissa's murder.

Sascha quickly put her shoes back on and ran to the front of their house, with Devon following behind her. Exiting the front entrance of their property, the Montagues were met with police lights and multiple police cars. Sascha rushed across the street to ask what was happening, only to witness Anna being taken out of her house in handcuffs. As tears streamed down her face, Anna turned to Sascha and said, "I did not do this."

Sascha stood by helplessly as she watched her friend being driven away in the back of a police car.

CHAPTER 18

Two days later Sascha was still reeling from Anna's arrest. It was gut-wrenching to watch her friend being led out in handcuffs and put into the back of a police car. Anna had been completely distraught, and no one could do a thing to help her in that moment. The only saving grace was that her girls were not home when the arrest happened. The twins were out with their father, Tomas, but Tomas had received multiple calls and texts from Anna's staff about the police being at the residence. Tomas then reached out to Sascha, hoping she could go check things out.

Sascha did not believe for one second that Anna was guilty of what she was being accused of and would help and support her friend in any way possible. Anna was still being held in jail, as her arraignment hearing had yet to be set, which Sascha found odd. Gina Campbell had been charged with the murder of Sascha's ex-husband Lucas, the attempted murder of Sascha and Anna, as well as charged with the kidnapping of Anna's twin daughters. Still, with all the heinous crimes Gina had committed, she had been provided an arraignment within forty-eight hours of her arrest, which Sascha understood to be the law.

Something was going on with Anna's arrest and the charges against her, and with so many powerful, potential suspects, it was no surprise there were some irregularities with the process. The shenanigans taking place just confirmed Sascha's belief that Anna was innocent, and now Sascha was starting to think she was being set up to take the fall for Marissa's murder. Anna was the most vulnerable resident in the Swell community when it came to finances, status, and connections. Tomas's medical device companies were being sued, and he had fallen from grace with many sex-related allegations from former students, employees, and colleagues.

Sascha would help her friend, but she needed to figure out how to first, and in order to do that, she would need more information, which led her to Anna's ex-husband. Tomas had temporarily moved back into the house across the street to be with his twin daughters while Anna was in custody. Sascha planned on paying him a visit this afternoon, not only to get information on how Anna was doing but to also question him under the guise of helping Anna since he was on her list of possible suspects. While Sascha sat watching Danielle play with her toy blocks, she sent a text to Tomas, asking if she could stop over for a short visit while her young daughter was napping. He agreed, which gave Sascha a sigh of relief.

An hour later, Sascha tapped on Devon's office door and popped her head in to let him know where she was going. He looked as if he was going to object, but instead he requested she take Matt with her. Nodding her head she told him she loved him and departed. Grabbing the two casseroles and a tray of brownies Sascha had asked her chef to make for the Greens, Sascha went over the questions she wanted to ask

Tomas in her head. Placing the food in a large tote bag for easier transport, she headed across the street with Matt in tow.

One of the twin daughters, Kimberly, answered the door and wrapped her arms around Sascha when she saw her. Sascha's heart ached for what the young girls must be going through. She reminded herself to check in on them more frequently throughout this process as Anna had no family close by, and Tomas had no relatives in the country.

"Hi, sweetie! I brought some of your favorites from Chef Janelle. Could you please take these to the kitchen and tell your father I am here?"

Sascha went and sat in the living room and waited for Tomas. When he appeared he looked distraught and disheveled and smelled of alcohol. This was not the Tomas Green that Sascha was used to seeing. The Tomas Green she knew was arrogant, confident, and always exceptionally groomed, but the man standing before her appeared broken.

"Tomas, thank you for agreeing to meet with me. How are you doing?"

"Not good," he responded, and started to cry. "Anna didn't do this. She would never do this."

Sascha was surprised by the emotional display from Tomas. Based how Anna described him over the years, and Sascha's own prior interactions with Tomas, he was a controlled, unemotional man. She did not want to accuse him of faking being distraught, but something about the display she was seeing felt off.

"I don't think she did what they are accusing her of either, and that is why I am here. Tell me what Anna needs, and I will help her in any way I can."

Tomas's eyes brightened at Sascha's words.

"Mrs. Montague, can I be frank with you?" Tomas asked, and as he flashed his smile, Sascha braced herself for an attempt at manipulation. Tomas was a good-looking man, but not at all the type of man Sascha would be attracted to, but that did not stop him from suddenly trying to charm her.

"Tomas, let me be clear. I am here for Anna. We need to get her out of jail. Why is she still in there?" Sascha demanded.

"I don't know why."

How could he not know why, Sascha thought. He was considered to be a brilliant man, yet he had no idea why his ex-wife had not been arraigned yet.

"What is her lawyer saying?" Sascha asked, barely containing her frustration.

"Well, her public defender isn't very—"

"Wait, why does she have a public defender?"

"Money is a little tight right now, and I have several lawsuits I'm currently dealing with, so—"

Sascha put her hand up to Tomas to get him to stop talking while she walked away to make a phone call. After speaking on the phone for several minutes, she hung up and returned to Tomas to continue their conversation.

"Devon and I will take care of the legal representation for Anna. Will you be able to handle her bail?"

"Yes, of course. And on behalf of Anna and our girls, we appreciate all of your help."

Sascha nodded and stood to depart.

"I'm not a bad guy, just so you know. I have made some bad choices, a lot of bad choices actually, but I do love her."

Sascha took her leave of the Green residence, torn about her interaction with Tomas.

～

"So let me get this straight—he did not have the money to hire a lawyer for her. How is that possible?" Devon asked, surprised at Sascha's words.

"Yes, apparently he's broke. Multiple lawsuits against his medical devices and businesses have caused his financial ruin. Add to that all the money he lost in his divorce to Anna and child support, and now a multimillion-dollar legal defense needed for her potential murder trial. It's all adding up in a big way."

"Wow, all the secrets and lies," Devon said, shaking his head.

"Yes, sounds like a juicy novel I would want to read, but unfortunately, this is my friend's life."

"So what happens next?" Devon inquired.

"I spoke with Braden Van Olsen, and he is going to meet with Anna this afternoon at the jail and assured me they would get her a bail hearing no later than tomorrow and that she should be out by tomorrow night."

"Well, that's good news," Devon said as she handed Sascha a glass of wine. "You're a good friend to Anna. She's very lucky to have you."

"Devon, I believe with every fiber of my being that she is innocent, and from the looks of what's been happening, I think she may have been set up from the beginning."

"Who would set her up, and why?" Devon asked.

"I haven't the foggiest idea. That's what makes this all such a big mystery," Sasha responded, and she sipped her wine.

"Sascha," Devon started with a tone that filled Sascha with dread. "While I completely support you supporting Anna, and I don't mind us paying for her defense, I want you to be careful, Nancy Drew. I know you're like a dog with a bone sometimes," Devon said, giving Sascha a stern look.

Sascha chuckled and said, "You joke, Mr. Montague, but I

do think I may have missed my calling at being a journalist, more specifically an investigative journalist."

"Maybe. And you are a brilliant woman and could do anything you set your mind to, but I just ask that you leave this investigation to the professionals."

"Sure," Sascha said as she refilled her wine glass.

Devon gave her an intense stare but did not push the issue, and Sascha did not say another word because she had no intentions of making any promises.

CHAPTER 19

Arriving at the ranch, Sascha felt exhausted already. She wanted to be excited about spending time with the girls for a few days at her stunning Montana property, and she was excited, but she also wanted to just sleep. She had been dragging lately and knew she needed to give her body the rest it craved. Between motherhood, writing, hunting Michael, consulting on the television show being made based on her books, and her husband's insatiable appetite for her in the bedroom, Sascha was burning the candle at both ends.

Sascha intentionally scheduled plenty of downtime in their three-day weekend trip to give herself a break from hosting, but she knew the girls would enjoy all she had in store for them. She planned for horseback riding, white water rafting at Yellowstone Park, and a wine and paint party at the house with a French chef on staff the entire visit. Thinking about all that she had arranged for the trip satisfied Sascha but also made her wish she could just send Cate and Sabrina off to enjoy it all on their own while she stayed in bed.

Both Sabrina and Cate walked in with their bags and caught Sascha in the middle of a yawn.

"How are you still tired, Sascha? You slept on the plane and barely stayed awake in the car ride from the hangar to here. What is going on with you?" Cate asked with a curious look on her face.

"I'm exhausted. Mentally and physically exhausted. The search for Michael and just knowing he is still out there is so stressful. Besides that I am not sleeping well…again." Sascha got emotional, and her eyes welled up.

Matt walked in with his bags just as the women were gathering around to hug Sascha. Matt looked at Sascha's teary face and apologized for interrupting them before excusing himself to put his bags away and start his security checks.

Watching him walk away, Sascha wiped her eyes and turned to her sister. "Matt is so sweet, and not to mention extremely attractive. Are you sure you don't want to give things with him another chance?"

"No, I'm sure. I think that ship has sailed."

Sascha made eye contact with Cate to prompt her input, but instead Cate focused her eyes elsewhere, making it clear she was staying out of this one.

Sascha wanted to pry more because she felt like she had never received the whole story about their breakup from her sister, but she knew she needed to bide her time on this topic for now, and then she could eventually flush out the truth.

A few hours later, after a long, hot bath and a short nap, a revived Sascha joined her sister and friend in the great room. They were playing cards, listening to eighties music, and drinking margaritas.

"Looks like I've been missing all the fun," Sascha said as she walked into the room. "I'm going to go check in with the chef and see what time dinner will be ready, but when I come back, I want to be dealt in."

"Then you had better hurry your butt back, Sleeping Beauty," Cate chided, and Sascha grabbed a handful of tortilla chips from a table of snacks on her way to the kitchen.

Sascha returned minutes later to announce that dinner would be ready in a half hour and joined the ladies for a game of gin rummy.

The women laughed and bantered, and just as Sabrina called out *rummy*, a staff member informed them dinner was ready to be served. As the women headed to the dining room, they passed Matt in the hallway, who appeared to have just finished working out. Matt was a catch. He was gorgeous; in fact he looked like he stepped off a fashion runway. But more importantly, he was kind and sweet, and he was patient. Matt would soon be launching his own private security firm, backed by Devon, but in the meantime, he would stay on as Sascha's personal bodyguard.

Matt stepped off to the side and gave a head nod in acknowledgment as they walked by. Sascha was once again reminded that she wanted to dig a little deeper into the Sabrina and Matt breakup and decided dinner tonight was the time to do it.

The women were seated for what was to be a simple four-course French meal. The first course was a consommé. It was light, delicious, and perfect for the cool Montana night. As the women sipped their soup, Sascha looked around, debating how to casually bring up Matt to Sabrina. Fortunately she did not have to wait long, thanks to Cate.

"What time are we starting out on the horseback riding trip tomorrow?" Cate asked.

"Tentatively around 9:00 a.m. Matt is going to go out to the trail and do some security checks first. Once he radios Tom that everything is safe, we will join him," Sascha stated.

"Oh, that sounds a little scary. Should he be going by himself?" Sabrina questioned with a concerned expression on her face.

"He won't be going alone. He will be accompanied by two of the ranch workers as well, but both he and Tom cannot be away from me at the same time," Sascha said as their soup bowls were cleared. While the second course of salads with a light vinaigrette was served, the women remained quiet. Once they were alone again, Sascha started in on Sabrina.

"You seem really concerned about Matt's well-being. I thought you were over him," Sascha started and saw her sister tense up and put her fork down.

"Are you not going to let this go?" Sabrina asked in frustration.

"No, I'm not. I love you, and I really like Matt, and I would love to see you both happy, and if that were together, that would be amazing," Sascha said, refusing to drop the topic.

"Sascha, I broke up with Matt because even though he liked me, he is in love with someone else," Sabrina said, and then started vigorously attacking her salad with the fork.

"In love with someone else? I have not seen Matt with anyone or even going out on dates. He's pretty focused on this job and working on his business plan and sparring with me," Sascha replied, finding Sabrina's statement hard to believe.

Sabrina and Cate made eye contact with each other, and then both turned to stare at Sascha intensely.

"Oh," Sascha said. "I see. Well, I can understand how it can look with how much time we spend together that someone could think that feelings could develop from that, but I look at Matt like a friend."

"Sure, that's how you see him. But when he and I were

dating, I saw him looking at you in a way that he never looked at me. I knew I had to end it. I saw how much he coveted you, and when I confronted him about it, he didn't deny it."

"He admitted he had feelings for me?"

"No, but no answer was the answer," Sabrina said, eyeing her sister with a serious expression.

"So what do I do?" Sascha asked, looking from Sabrina to Cate.

"Sweetie, you don't need to do anything. He's a good guy and would never try to hurt what you and Devon have. He is probably staying around until Michael is no longer a threat, and then he will be off running his new business. Unless he does or says something inappropriate or starts to make you feel uncomfortable, which is not likely to happen, just let it be," Cate said.

Sascha nodded her head in agreement. She would never want to make Matt uncomfortable by bringing the topic up, and she was not sure how Devon would react if he found out. After everything Michael has put them through, Sascha doubted Devon would tolerate another man in their lives who had feelings for her.

By the time the third course was served, Sascha was feeling anxious. The third course consisted of delicious roasted chicken and thick-cut french fries, which were Sascha's favorite. Sascha had requested an extra basket of fries for the table, which was needed because fries were her comfort food, and she needed that right now. Sascha indulged in the food and ignored all the thoughts whirling around in her head.

For the final course, crème brûlée was served, and the women decided to take the dessert outside by a large outdoor fireplace. The evening air and nearly full moon calmed Sascha. She relaxed with a glass of wine and soon began to yawn. She was once again exhausted and knew it was time to go to bed.

"Okay, ladies, it is time for me to go to bed," Sascha said as she stood up. "And please feel free to talk about me while I'm gone," she said with a chuckle as she started walking away.

"Don't worry, we will," Cate called after her while laughing.

Sascha woke up the next morning surprised at how great she slept the first night at the ranch, considering all she had on her mind when she went to bed. She took a long, hot shower, got dressed, and then video chatted with Devon and Danielle for a bit before going to get something to eat. She skipped her normal workout since they would be on horseback for most of the day, and she was already dealing with fatigue.

The women set out on horseback with Matt, Tom, a trail guide, and their equestrian expert in tow. A little over a year ago, Sascha and Devon purchased the nearly two-hundred-acre property and the ranch on it. The property boasted a creek, lush trees, trails, and rolling hills. It was a magnificent sight, and the group was able to ride for hours and never leave the Montague Ranch.

They stopped for a lunch break, a much-needed rest for the horses, and rest for the women who were not used to being in saddles for extended periods of time. When Sascha sat down in the grassy area to enjoy one of the delectable sandwiches the chef had prepared for the group, her bottom ached. She quickly began to dread getting back in the saddle, but once they were done with lunch, they would begin their return trip.

Sascha was sweaty and dirty and in wonderful spirits when she returned home from the day out on the trails with her friends. Everyone needed a shower and hurried off to their rooms once they entered the home. Sascha checked in with the chef before going off to her room, and dinner would be ready in less than an hour, which was perfect because she could not wait to sit down for dinner that night. Sascha entered her room, put her phone on the charger, and began to undress. Getting into the shower, Sascha took her time and let the powerful showerheads massage her achy body.

Exiting the shower Sasha wrapped a towel around her body and sat on the bed as she moisturized her skin. As she rubbed body cream over her arms, her phone rang, and she reached to grab it, surprised to find it off the charger. She could have sworn she had placed it on the charger but disregarded that thought as she picked up the phone from the nightstand to take Devon's call.

"Hi, honey!" Sascha excitedly said to her husband. "I miss you."

Sascha and Devon chatted until she looked at her watch and realized it was dinnertime. Agreeing she would call him back after dinner, Sascha quickly dressed and went out to join the ladies for dinner. Enjoying cocktails and snacks, they both looked at Sascha when she entered the room and said, "Finally."

"My apologies, let's go eat."

The women were famished from their earlier excursion, and the chef provided the perfect comforting and filling meal to satisfy even the pickiest eater. The evening's meal consisted of coq au vin, creamy mashed potatoes, haricot verts, and fresh baked French bread. The meal was paired with a pinot noir and was hands down the best meal Sascha had ever had.

Conversation that evening was light and filled with talk about books, movies, and celebrity gossip. They were all tired from a day of activity out in the sun and were looking forward to turning in early. They said their good nights and went to their rooms to turn in. Sascha changed into her pajamas, did her nighttime beauty routine, and then called Devon and Danielle. After getting off the phone with her loved ones, Sascha turned on the television, climbed into bed, and promptly fell asleep.

Sascha was sleeping peacefully that night until she felt something crawling on her arm. She woke up in the middle of the night to find her room pitch-black, which was odd since she had fallen asleep with the television on. Rubbing her arm to make sure nothing was there, she reached to turn on her nightstand lamp, but nothing happened. The power was out. Sascha laid there for a moment, debating whether or not she should get up to wake the house manager or just let it be. Her fatigue won out. She was still tired and just wanted to continue to slumber. Turning over she tried to go back to sleep, but suddenly the hairs stood up on the back of her neck. Her instincts told her she was not alone in her room. Sitting up Sascha listened as her heart pounded in her ears.

"Is someone there?" she called out into the dark. She heard not a peep. Telling herself she was just being silly, she again turned over, but as she lay quietly, still awake, a familiar scent in the room drew her attention. Reaching for her cell phone on the nightstand, she quickly pressed the flashlight button on her device and faced the bright light in the direction of her bedroom door. At first she saw nothing, and just as she was about to chastise herself for being para-noid, she spotted a goggled figure hiding in the corner of the room. Screaming at the top of her lungs, Sascha jumped out of her bed as the figure took off out of the bedroom. She ran after them, yelling for Matt as she did so.

Matt exited his room with a gun in hand as they both began pursuit through the dark house and out into the night. As Sascha ran out across a field, Matt grabbed her arm and forced her to stop.

"What are you doing? Let go of me," Sascha demanded as she stared angrily at Matt.

"This is likely a trap to lure you out here in the dark and take you. It's not safe. We need to go back."

Sascha hated to admit it, but Matt was likely right. It was a trap.

"Damn it!" she yelled as she marched back to the house in frustration.

As Sascha and Matt walked back to the house, the power came back on, and the property lit up. Standing on the large wraparound porch were Cate, Sabrina, and Tom and the house manager, who were both holding weapons in their hands.

"What happened?" Cate asked as she and the group followed Matt and Sascha back into the house.

Entering the house, Matt locked the front door, and he and the house manager took off to different wings of the house with their weapons drawn while Tom stayed with Sascha. Watching them walk away, Sascha turned back to Sabrina and Cate.

"Michael happened. He was in my room."

"What?" Cate and Sabrina said in unison.

"Michael was here? You saw him?" Cate asked with both fear and anger in her voice.

"Well no. I just saw a figure, but I smelled Michael."

"What does that even mean? You smelled him?"

"I sensed someone was in the room but started to doubt myself. But then I realized there was a familiar scent in my room. A scent that Michael always wears. It's like a combination of cedar, spice, and arrogance."

"I remember that scent all too well. I will never forget it," Cate said as she pulled her robe tighter around her body.

"House is clear, and with the power back on, all perimeter

and house alarms and cameras are once again operational," Matt stated as he returned to the women.

"Great because I am going back to bed," Sascha said as she yawned and started for her room.

"Really, just like that, Sascha?" Sabrina asked in shock.

"Yeah, just like that," Sascha stated, turning to face her sister. "Michael is not coming back tonight, and if he planned on taking me tonight, I think he would have made more of an effort. He just wanted to see me and to touch me or something, and since he did both of those things tonight, he will not be back for a while."

"Wow, I'm not gonna lie. If I were you, I would be freaking out right now," Sabrina said.

"Who says I'm not freaking out inside?" Sascha said, and she walked off.

Five minutes later as Sascha lay in her bed, she heard her sister come into her room and crawl into bed with her.

"Good night, sissy," Sabrina said to her big sister.

"Night," Sascha replied, happy her sister was there.

CHAPTER 20

aking up the following morning, Sascha
found Devon sitting in the kitchen of their
Montana ranch. Seeing her husband made her burst into
tears with relief and comfort. Devon held Sascha tightly.
After minutes of shedding tears, Sascha pulled back and sat
in the chair next to him.

"I take it Matt called you?"

"He did, but it should have been you," Devon said in a
firm tone.

"I know, but it was the middle of the night, and you were
in California, and I'm here. I mean, what could I expect you
to do? Hop on a plane in the middle of the night and fly here
to comfort your poor, frightened wife?" Sascha finished her
last sentence with more tears.

"Of course I am going to get on a plane day or night, no
matter where you are or what I'm doing. You are my fair
maiden, and I will always come running to the rescue."

"My Prince Charming," Sascha teased, and she leaned in
to kiss his lips, then pulled back. "By the way, Prince, where
is my child?"

"Danielle is safe with your dad and Maggie and Lena at our house."

"Good."

"Now tell me what happened last night."

Sascha recounted the night's events to Devon, and as she did so, she remembered additional details.

"I was woken up because in my dream something was touching or crawling on my arm, but I now realize it was a hand. He was standing over me as I slept, wearing night vision goggles. He must have been touching my arm, and that is what woke me up."

"This is maddening," Devon exclaimed as he raked his fingers through his hair.

"It is, but I do see the silver lining in what happened last night."

"How so?"

"Being on the run is taking its toll on him, and he can't keep doing this much longer."

"While I agree with you, it also means he is becoming desperate and reckless and completely unpredictable."

"I don't care. I just want this over and done with because I cannot live like this anymore," Sascha said vehemently.

Pulling her back into his arms, Devon held his wife while he gently rubbed her back.

"Ready to go home?" he asked after a few moments.

"This is our home too, but it seems like Michael is managing to ruin every trip, every vacation, and has eyes and ears everywhere," Sascha replied in frustration.

"Almost like he has someone in our inner circle watching us and reporting everything?"

"Yes! Any thoughts on who the spy might be?" Sascha asked with a glint in her eyes.

Devon stayed quiet for several seconds before speaking. "I

have some ideas, but I want to keep my eye on things and see how they play out. Okay?"

Sascha was not really okay with her husband's response, but she felt too emotionally drained to get into it at the moment. Sascha felt frustrated and annoyed at her husband, and while she didn't use those words, her facial expression must have revealed her thoughts because her husband pulled her into his arms.

"When are you going to realize you are my everything and nothing and no one will ever change that?"

"I do realize it, and I love you," Sascha said, pulling her husband into a kiss.

"Good morning, lovebirds," Cate said, entering the kitchen. Grabbing a bottle of water from the fridge, Cate took a handful of supplements and chugged half the bottle, which made Sascha chuckle.

"So how crazy was last night?" Cate asked as she eyed Devon and Sascha.

"It was nuts. Like something out of a horror movie, and I am still trying to wrap my head around the fact that it actually happened."

"Well, he's clearly a complete psycho now, if he wasn't already, but thank God you woke up when you did," Cate stated in disgust.

"How are you doing, Cate? I'm sure it cannot be easy for you knowing he was in this house last night," Sascha said, as she walked around the kitchen island and put her arm around her friend.

"I hate him. I hate him so much. The thought of him fills me with so much rage, and I know that's me giving him power over my thoughts and emotions, but I cannot help it." Cate's pale, freckled face turned beet red as she spoke about Michael.

The group continued to discuss Michael as Matt and

Sabrina walked into the kitchen. Sascha sensed tension between the two and tried to make eye contact with her sister to get an idea of the issue, but Sabrina conveniently kept her eyes averted. Matt did, however, make eye contact with Sascha, and she saw sadness.

"I know I did not get a chance to say this last night, but thank you so much, Matt. You were right to stop me from running after Michael. You probably saved my life."

"Well, I wished I had stopped him from getting into the house in the first place," Matt responded, his frustration and disappointment clear.

Sascha only blamed one person for last night, and she had a feeling their game of cat and mouse was nearing its end.

CHAPTER 21

Sascha knocked on and opened the door to Devon's office to let him know it was time to eat. What she found was Delilah sitting on his desk taking notes while he read information from a report. Looking up from the papers in hand, Devon greeted his wife with a smile. Sascha coldly informed her husband it was time for dinner and left the room. Sascha started back to the kitchen, but she was so upset that the thought of food made her sick to her stomach. Instead she headed for her bedroom to lie down.

Ten minutes later Devon walked into the bedroom and asked her if she was feeling all right. Sascha lied and said she was just tired and continued to lie on the bed in the fetal position facing away from him. Devon went to lie on the bed beside her, then pulled her into his arms. "I love you," he whispered as he nuzzled her neck.

Sascha continued to lie there, stiff in her husband's arms, angry and frustrated that he seemed to be oblivious that his increased desires for her came from his hidden desires for Delilah.

"I want her fired," Sascha blurted out, no longer able to hide her anger and jealousy.

"You want who fired?" Devon asked as he sat up with a confused expression on his face.

Sascha turned over and gave her husband a look of frustration and said, "Delilah, that's who."

"Okay, she's gone. May I ask why you want me to fire her, though?"

"Because I don't trust her," Sascha responded.

Devon made a face but didn't say anything.

"Wait, what was that face for?" Sascha asked.

"I just expected you to say something else," Devon said.

"Like what?" Sascha asked, confused.

"That the spy is Delilah. I have always been suspicious of her," Devon replied nonchalantly.

"What? Then why did we hire her, and why didn't you say anything before now?" Sascha asked, surprised by Devon's declaration.

"Sweetheart, I do not want to play the blame game, but if you remember, I didn't even want to interview her."

"But Emma recommended her."

"Did she, though? Something has always felt off about that letter from Emma."

"You don't think it was from Emma?"

"At the time I did. I was so grief-stricken I was not thinking clearly. I didn't want to even think about replacing Emma, but then I thought if this is what Emma suggests and with your support, maybe it was the right thing to do. Then I met her, she seemed studious and affable, and I thought okay I can work with her. But it was not before long I started to see the changes. The sexy outfits. The flirty behavior and the meanness toward the other staff members. She was a fraud and up to no good, but the question was to what end. Did she work for a business competitor? Was she looking to compromise me for blackmail purposes? Or maybe she was hoping to break up our marriage and marry herself a wealthy man. I have seen it all over the years, so they were all possibilities. But her being a Michael plant was not on my radar, and it should have been."

Sascha stated, "I had a pit in the bottom of my stomach the day we hired her. My gut said something was off, but my pride kept me from admitting I felt jealous and threatened by her."

"So is it that you don't trust her or you don't trust me?" Devon's facial expression told Sascha his feelings were wounded by the implication.

"I trust you, but you cannot deny that since she has become your assistant, you have become extra lusty. You have always had a healthy appetite for sex, but lately you cannot get enough of me. What's changed then if it's not her?"

Devon took a deep breath and then took his wife's hand in his. "There's something I need to tell you."

When Sascha heard those words, she thought she was going to faint. She closed her eyes and regulated her breathing. *Deep breaths*, she coaxed herself. "Okay, what is it?" Sascha asked, fearing the worst.

"I have started seeing someone."

Sascha felt as if she had been punched in the gut but sat silently, resisting the urge to snatch her hand back from her husband.

"I thought I was fine after the Michael incident, but the fear of losing you became overwhelming. I did not want to let you out of my sight. I couldn't sleep, and when I traveled, I watched the home cameras nonstop. I saw how overprotective and controlling I was becoming, and I did not like that person. I could not be that person," Devon paused as Sascha started to realize exactly who he had started seeing.

"I never thought I was the type of guy who would ever go to therapy, but now I guess I am, and it has helped."

Sascha exhaled, breathing a sigh of relief.

"You look relieved. Are you not surprised?" Devon questioned.

"No, I am surprised, but I just was not sure where the conversation was going. Honestly I was terrified when you said you had started seeing someone."

"Ah, yes. I can see how those words could cause alarm for a wife."

"So tell me about this therapist."

"Dr. Price is fantastic. She has been a therapist for over forty years and reminds me of Emma a little bit. The great thing about our sessions is that she is patient but has forced me out of my comfort zone. Dealing with the abandonment of my father and the loss of my mother and now the near-constant fear of losing you. It has been a struggle."

Sascha's eyes streamed tears as she realized Devon had been holding all of his pain in and being strong for her, but recent events had brought it all to the surface.

"I'm so sorry that I have not been a more comforting and supportive wife for you," Sascha said as she leaned in and hugged her husband.

Pulling back, Devon looked into Sascha's eyes and said, "You are my ideal woman. You are my best friend, you are my confidant, and you have given me a life so wonderful that I am not sure I deserve it."

Leaning back into Sascha, Devon placed a soft kiss on her lips before she pulled away this time.

"Okay, now I know you are seeing a therapist, but how has that made you so horny recently?" Sascha asked, still needing the change in his sexual appetite addressed.

Devon laughed heartily as Sascha looked on.

"I didn't realize my friskiness was a problem but—"

"It is most certainly not a problem," Sascha interrupted. "I just wanted to make sure a certain new sexy assistant wasn't the reason for my amazing sex life."

"Of course not, and I thought we always had amazing sex. In fact, it is taking all my restraint right now not to flip you over and take you." Devon's green eyes glowed with desire, which made Sascha's heart rate increase. Devon continued his explanation as Sascha started unbuttoning his shirt.

"I cannot pinpoint what has changed, but my therapist told me to lean into all my feelings. My fears, my anger, my sadness, and my jealousy."

Sascha stopped undoing Devon's pants to ask, "What jealousy?"

"All the men worshipping you. It's maddening. You're *my* wife. So instead of continuing to get jealous of all the men who want you, I appreciate the fact that you chose me. And I show that appreciation by loving you, by making love to you, and by making you scream out in ecstasy."

Sascha smiled softly at Devon's words. Standing up, she slid out of her panties, hiked up her dress, and then straddled Devon and rode him with hot passion. Devon leaned his head back as his wife took control and murmured for him to cum for her. Devon grabbed Sascha's hips tightly as he thrust upward until they both cried out in pleasure.

"I think I really like this Dr. Price," Sascha said as she laid against her husband, totally spent.

CHAPTER 22

Sascha, Devon, Sabrina, and Cate all arrived together in Los Angeles to attend the premiere event for the Coven of Plumvale television series. Tatum, Tom, and Drew were also traveling with them, while Danielle stayed back at the Swell with her grandparents, Lena, and Matt. Sascha and Devon decided not to fire Delilah just yet, but Sascha made sure Delilah was nowhere near her home or their event while she and Devon were out of town. Matt was left behind to ensure Danielle's and her grandparents' safety.

The moment they landed, Sascha's anxiety went into overdrive. She was terribly nervous about her fans' reception of the Coven television series. The fans loved the books, and there was a cult following of the book series. But she wondered, *Would they love the television adaptation too?* She wanted them to like it and enjoy seeing their favorite characters come to life, but she was expecting some of the Coven "purists" to take issue with deviations for the source material. Both the books and the television scripts had been labors of love for Sascha, although she had a lot less control with the show than she did with the books. While some changes were made to create some surprises for the viewers, the changes were likely to irritate some fans.

"Oh my gosh, Sascha, you look like you're going to be sick," Cate commented as the elevator doors opened.

"That's because I am," Sascha said, and she rushed into the penthouse, looking for the nearest bathroom.

Devon followed his wife to the bathroom and asked her if she was all right. She nodded her head as she flushed the toilet and wiped her mouth with tissue paper.

"Okay. Do you need anything?"

Sitting on the bathroom floor, she responded, "Nerves of steel and a ginger ale please."

"Coming right up, with a ginger ale that is." Devon left and quickly returned to find Sascha still sitting on the floor.

"What's really going on?" he asked as he handed her a drink.

"Do you ever feel like you don't deserve to be where you're at in life? Like all of your success is just some big fluke, and you don't belong in the billionaire's club or in the Swell?"

"Ah, so the impostor's syndrome rears its ugly head. It's about time," Devon said as he sat down next to her.

"About time? Do you think I'm an impostor?" Sascha asked with hurt in her voice.

"No, sweetheart, quite the opposite in fact. I think you're amazing. You have been incredibly successful, and you're always so sure of yourself. I was starting to think you were superhuman. You have a brilliant financial mind and could have crushed the financial world if you wanted to, but you decided to give it all up to be a writer, and then boom, you're great at that too. Meanwhile us mere mortals are filled with self-doubt and insecurities while my wife, a goddess among us, makes it all look so easy."

"Aww, I love you," Sascha said as Devon stood up and then helped her to her feet. "Okay, I can do this."

"You got this, baby."

~

LEAVING the hotel that evening to attend the premiere event, Sascha was feeling calmer and more confident than she had earlier that day. That was until their limousine pulled up to the red carpet. Sascha was unprepared for the amount of press and people who would be in attendance at the premiere. The flashing lights from the cameras and people screaming both her and Devon's names when they exited the vehicle was panic-attack inducing. As they walked the red carpet, Devon seemed to sense her uncomfortableness and gripped her hand for support. As the couple stopped and posed for a picture, Sascha looked up lovingly to her husband, capturing his gaze, as she silently thanked him for being her real-life knight in a black tie. Sascha fought the urge to lock lips with her husband since there were so many eyes on them.

Although Sascha was feeling skittish about the audience's reception of her book turned television show, she felt completely confident in how she presented that evening. With her big curls loose, Sascha wore a white, tea-length, form-fitting dress with a sweetheart neckline. Her look was completed with smoky eyes, crimson lips, and a simple diamond pendant necklace, gifted to her by Devon.

"You look so hot," her husband whispered while they posed for more pictures.

As the couple moved on along the red carpet, with Cate and Sabrina trailing behind, Sascha dreaded her first stop at a reporter. Fortunately all questions being asked were about her writing, the series, and about working with Marcus

Winters. Sascha breathed a sigh of relief that she received no questions about Michael. After making it through the crush of reporters incident free, inside the theater, the group found their seats, and Sascha stared down the row at Cate, whom she noticed was sitting next to Marcus and flirting with him. They actually appeared to be a couple.

Sascha could not believe her eyes. Marcus was a wonderful, sweet man, but he was also short and chubby and eccentric and not at all Cate's type. Sascha caught Cate's eye, and her friend winked at her. Sascha could not help but smile in return, but Cate was getting grilled later. Sascha wanted details.

As the presentation started, the producers and Marcus all spoke to the audience about the project, then Sascha was called up, and the audience cheered for her. After thanking them all for coming out and supporting the series, and their continued fight for the Coven of Plumvale to be made into a movie and television series, she passed the mic over as the actors were introduced. When the lights went dark, Sascha leaned over and kissed Devon.

"I have been wanting to do that all night."

The premiere had been a success, and Sascha felt like a huge weight had been lifted off her shoulders. Although there were some unhappy fans, which was expected, most of the reviews were good, and the overall reception of the series was great. The plan was for each of her books to be covered over a season, which meant there would be at least three more seasons of the Coven of Plumvale. Which also meant there would be pressure on her to finish future books in the series faster. Sascha's fifth book was nearly complete, but she did not want to feel pressured to write faster, fearing that pressure would stifle her creativity and negatively impact the quality of her books.

The following morning Sascha sat with Cate at the penthouse's dining table, sipping her coffee and listening to Cate as she gave her scoop on everything she missed after leaving the after-party, including Sabrina making out with an A-list celebrity. Sascha and Devon had attended the party but left early, both preferring to go back to the hotel and relax. Sascha did stay at the party long enough to see Cate and Marcus coupled up, and she still had so many questions, which Cate promised to answer.

Just as the topic changed to Marcus, Tatum walked in with a magazine in hand and sat it on the table in front of Sascha.

"What is this?" Sascha asked, picking up the magazine.

The magazine had run an article with Sascha and Devon on the cover with the headline saying this was what having it all looked like. The picture was perfect. They made a gorgeous couple, but with Michael on the loose, Sasha had a dark cloud hanging over her life. They were never completely at ease and were always on alert. This was no way to live, and no one should envy her circumstances.

"This was just last night. How in the world did they produce a magazine that fast?" Sascha asked in surprise.

"It was probably all ready to go; they just needed pictures from the premiere event," Cate said.

"Well, I hate the headline. People who do not have a lot of money often believe that with money comes happiness," Sascha said to the two women as she put the magazine back down.

"Doesn't it, though?" Sabrina chided as she walked into the room.

"Have you met my neighbors at the Swell?" Sascha responded, rolling her eyes.

Sabrina walked over, picked up the magazine, and said, "Wow, you two look so good. And, Sascha, surely you realize how you hit the jackpot with a man like Devon. All the money, my adorable niece, and all of your success, right?"

"Or course I do, but it also all came with a high cost," Sascha said, shaking her head.

"Everything has a cost. The question is, are you willing to pay it to have what you want?" Cate said, and she began flipping through the magazine.

Sascha was sitting quietly, deep in thought, when her phone vibrated. Picking it up to read the text, Sascha slammed the phone back down moments later after reading a taunting text clearly from Michael.

"What is it?" Cate asked.

"It's the cost," Sascha said as she stood up and walked away.

CHAPTER 23

Sascha glanced up from her computer to find her husband standing in the doorway. She was so engrossed in her writing that she did not even hear the door open. Devon entered Sascha's office with a look of urgency on his face and a manila package in hand. Closing the door behind him, he walked over to her desk and placed the envelope down and said, "We found him."

Sascha ripped open the envelope to find pictures of Michael entering a home, getting in and out of cars, and sitting in restaurants.

"Where is this?"

"Montenegro."

"Okay, well, let's go get that bastard," Sascha said as she stood up to go start preparing for their trip.

"I love it that my wife is such as badass," Devon said as he observed his wife, while flames of passion lit his green eyes.

Before Sascha could walk away, Devon pulled her into a hot, steamy kiss. Sascha returned his kiss with intense passion as his hands slid up her dress and into her panties. Sascha moaned as her hands went for his belt buckle and undid his pants. Lifting Sascha up onto her desk, Devon entered her with urgency. Sascha wrapped her legs around his hips as she pulled their bodies closer together, wanting him deeper inside her. Their eyes locked in a vivid moment before Devon's lips continued down to kiss Sascha's neck, face, and then back to her lips before their bodies shook, finding their release.

"Wow, that was so good," Sascha whispered in Devon's ear, before he kissed her once more.

By the time Sascha made it upstairs, she only had one hour to quickly shower, dress, pack a bag, and be on her way to the hangar with Devon. Sascha took care of business in record time. She met with Lena to leave instructions with her for Danielle and spoke with Sabrina, who would be staying at the Montague residence to help with Danielle while they were gone.

Their flight took off an hour later, and by the time Sascha and Devon were in the air, they were serious and focused on the task at hand. Sascha was reading everything she could find on Montenegro. Montenegro was a beautiful country that she would have liked to visit under normal circumstances. Montenegro was a southeastern European country, located in the Balkans. And while it was a stunning country, it was clear that Michael chose the country for its lack of extradition treaty with the United States, which was why the Montagues had a plan. While Sascha reviewed maps and familiarized herself with the country and the area Michael was supposedly located in, Devon spoke with the FBI at their international headquarters to alert them of Michael's whereabouts and to receive their assistance.

Thirteen and a half hours later, Sascha and Devon landed in Kotor, Montenegro. Stepping off the plane, the group was met with cool temperatures, and Sascha's stiff body felt even worse. In spite of feeling terrible, Sascha wanted to go after

Michael immediately upon landing, but Devon disagreed, and Sascha knew he was right. Their intelligence on Michael was stale at this point, and reconnaissance would need to be conducted to ensure they were not walking into a trap, especially in completely unfamiliar territory.

Plus the FBI had asked them to hold off while they made contacts locally and got a team in place, which made Sascha uncomfortable. Michael had contacts everywhere, and the more people who knew about the Montagues' presence in Montenegro and a plan to capture him, the more likely the mission would be compromised, and Michael would get away once again. Sascha trusted no one anymore when it came to Michael.

Arriving at their hotel, Sascha quickly showered and changed into comfortable clothes. Although she tried to calm and distract herself a bit, her heart was racing as a man came to their door and dropped off an envelope for Devon. The intel they had this time was strong, and Michael was believed to still be in the country, technically, but he was staying on a Montenegrin island by the name of Sveti Nikola. The island was remote, and they would only be able to get there by boat. Just thinking about it made Sascha's head hurt.

Sascha had been tired, but she was unable to sleep on the flight to Montenegro, and while she initially felt sluggish driving to their hotel, her adrenaline had started to kick in. They had several rooms they intended to use as their base camp to track Michael in the city. Sascha needed to be there to identify him for the authorities as Michael had changed his appearance. From the photos Sascha had seen, his hair, which he normally kept cut short, was much longer and darker. He had also grown out his facial hair and was thinner than usual, but it was definitely Michael. Sascha had no doubt of that.

Early the following morning, the Montagues received a

knock on their hotel room door. Devon got up to answer it, while Sascha lay in bed and heard the voice of the federal agent they had spoken to earlier in the evening.

"We'll meet you downstairs in ten minutes," Sascha heard her husband say.

Closing the door Devon turned to find Sascha out of bed and already getting dressed. Ten minutes later the couple entered the hotel lobby with both Matt and James in tow and met up with two FBI agents who were drinking coffee in to-go cups. It was still dark out when they left the hotel, heading to a small village just outside of town, which was where they would take a boat to Sveti Nikola. Coming from the direction of the village in the early morning hours would be less suspicious than coming from the main port.

Sascha hoped Michael was still sleeping when they arrived so they would have the element of surprise, but with Michael you never knew what to expect. The group went in two separate boats; both boats had a federal agent and two local police officers. The trip out to the island was nearly forty-five minutes long, and the temperature, especially out on the water, was freezing, but Sascha barely noticed. Her blood was boiling with the thought of them finally capturing Michael. Sascha could see the lights from the lighthouse as they approached. *Could this finally be over?* she thought as both boats pulled up and docked.

The sun was just starting to rise, and Sascha could finally see where they were at. Exiting the boats the local police led the way, while the federal agents, the Montagues, and the Montagues' security team followed behind them. The group took a trail from the beach that was expected to lead to the home Michael was allegedly staying at. When the group came to a clearing, Sascha was surprised by what she saw. It was a beautiful, large home that reminded her of their Orcas

Island home. As they slowly started their approach, they heard a loud noise in the distance.

"Is that what I think it is?" Sascha asked, looking to her husband.

"It's a goddamn helicopter. That son of a bitch knows we're here," he responded, and he took off running in the direction of the noise. The rest of the group followed in pursuit, but they were too late. They arrived just in time to see the helicopter lift off. As Sascha looked up, she saw Michael in the passenger seat of the helicopter staring intensely back at her. She stared furiously, hoping they would crash, and watched until the helicopter disappeared off into the distance.

The return trip back to the mainland was miserable. Sascha felt the icy wind on her face and body and rage in her heart. Returning to their hotel frustrated, Sascha wanted to scream. It was obvious at this point that Michael was taunting them and that they were going to have to do this on their own and not involve the authorities as someone in their midst could not be trusted. Clearly someone had tipped Michael off about their presence in Montenegro, and once again he was gone. Sascha did not think the leak was in her group, but there was a leak. Michael was a very wealthy man, and sadly, money could buy just about anything, including a federal agent.

Nearly two hours after they saw Michael fly off, the Montagues entered their hotel room, and Sascha immediately sensed something was off. Their room had been cleaned while they were out, even though the sun was barely up and there was a do-not-disturb sign on their door. *What maids are cleaning occupied rooms at seven in the morning?* Sascha thought. With her suspicions on high, Sascha kneeled down to her bag to check for missing items and quickly realized a couple of pairs of her underwear were missing. Sascha raked her hands through her hair as her anger raged.

"Baby, we will get him. I promise," Devon said as he came up behind her and rubbed her shoulders.

Sascha loved her husband but did not believe that he believed what he was saying. But she appreciated his efforts to comfort her anyway. Looking up at her husband to thank him, something caught her attention out of the corner of her eye. Turning, Sascha saw a white envelope with her name on it propped against the lamp on the nightstand on her side of the bed. Standing up Sascha rushed to grab the note as she had a sinking feeling it was from Michael.

Opening the envelope Sascha instantly recognized Michael's handwriting.

Sascha, why can't you just listen? Be in touch soon, my love. The note was signed by Michael.

Handing the note to Devon, Sascha saw his face turn red as fury took over. Deciding not to mention her missing undergarments, Sascha started packing the rest of her items and forming a plan in her mind on how to deal with Michael on her own.

CHAPTER 24

Sascha awoke in bed with bright light streaming through the windows. It was a Saturday morning, but she rarely slept in late, even on weekends. Turning over she found Devon's side of the bed empty. There would be no run or working out for her this morning. She felt too exhausted. Sitting up her whole body ached. She thought she might be coming down with something but threw on her robe and went downstairs instead of pulling the covers back over her head like she really wanted to do. Coffee should do the trick, or at least she hoped it would.

Walking into the kitchen, Sascha poured herself a cup of coffee and found Devon and Danielle playing with Bella in the backyard. Looking up, Danielle yelled, "Mommy," and ran to hug her mother, followed by an excited Bella wagging her tail.

"Oh, I see who's the favorite around here." Devon chuckled as he walked over to kiss his wife. "Ready for some breakfast?"

"Yes, I'm famished," Sascha responded while yawning.

"Still tired or are you not feeling well?" Devon asked, looking on with concern.

"A little tired but I think I just needed to get up and move around and have my coffee and some breakfast."

The family filled their plates and went to sit and enjoy breakfast in their sunny breakfast room. Sascha looked around, noticing the house seemed quieter than usual.

"Where is everyone at?" Sascha asked as she realized she had not seen any of their house staff that morning.

"I gave them all the day off. I figured it is such a beautiful day, they should all be out enjoying it."

"That's a wonderful idea, and I think we can fend for ourselves for a day," Sascha replied, and she yawned again.

"How about you rest today as well? You're clearly tired, and I think Danielle and I can take care of the dishes. After your nap maybe we can have some pool time or go for a walk out to the bluffs or trails."

Sascha considered arguing but thought better of it, kissed her husband and daughter, and then went back to bed for a few more hours. Waking up the second time, Sascha felt much more refreshed. She took a shower, got dressed, and went to find her family. Checking her watch, she knew it was nap time for Danielle, and Sascha peeked into her daughter's room and found her fast asleep. Going downstairs to find Devon, she found her husband watching a game on the television in the family room.

"Ah, look who's up. Feel better?"

"Much better," Sascha said as she took a seat next to her husband on the couch.

Sascha sat for a few more minutes before deciding she found sports on television to be horribly boring, although she loved attending games in person.

Standing up she informed Devon she was going to the kitchen to start prepping food for that night's dinner. After cheering to the recent score on the television, he paused the game and offered to help her.

"Thank you, but I got this. Enjoy the game," Sascha said, and she took the baby monitor from the table next to Devon and went off to the kitchen.

As Sascha chopped vegetables, she felt her phone vibrate in her back pocket. Wiping her hands on a kitchen towel, she pulled her phone out and glanced at the caller ID. Her phone showed it was her sister.

"Hey, Brina, what's up?" Sascha answered cheerily.

"I warned you not to look for me," a sinister voice said on the other end of the line.

"Michael?" Sascha asked in surprise, and she started quickly walking through her house, back to where Devon was located. Reaching her husband, she motioned to the phone and put it on speaker.

"I love how feisty you are. It's very sexy, but just remember, you brought this on yourself, love. I don't want to hurt you, but I did warn you."

"What is that supposed to mean, Michael? What are you planning to do?" Sascha asked, fearing the response.

"Just know that you forced my hand," Michael stated in an eerily calm voice.

"I will kill you with my bare hands if you touch a hair on her head," Devon raged.

"It isn't Sascha's head you need to be worried about," Michael responded, and the phone went dead.

Sascha hung up the phone and put her hand to her mouth. Shaking her head in disbelief, she sat down on the couch, picked up a throw pillow, and buried her face in it, letting out a scream of pure frustration and anger.

"I cannot believe he slipped through our fingers again, and this is still our life."

"We found him once, and we will find him again," Devon

said soothingly, but his wife did not believe he meant his words.

"Really? Because I'm starting to think this is going to be a case of luring him out of hiding rather than finding him. Michael is smart and clever, and he always has a backup plan for his backup plan. He will not be found unless he wants to be."

"So what are you saying?"

"I'm saying we know what he wants. Let's let him think he can have it."

"Sascha, he wants you, and there is no way in hell we are going to use you as bait. He's too unpredictable," Devon said, standing up and pacing.

"Listen, we don't need to make any decisions right now, but I think we are eventually going to need to talk about changing our strategy for dealing with Michael. But for now can you just come give me a hand with dinner?" Sascha did not really need help in the kitchen, but she knew Devon needed a distraction as much as she did. Otherwise he would just sit in the family room and stew over the phone call with Michael.

Before dinner they decided to go for a long family walk at the Swell along with their dog, Bella. Danielle loved to walk and explore nature, but the Montagues also brought along their daughter's little covered red wagon in case she got tired on the trail. The sun was shining brightly, but there was a coolness in the air along with a slight breeze that smelled of ocean and sea salt. The family chose to walk the forest trails rather than the bluffs as it was too chilly for their little one over by the water. The walking trails of the Swell's forest resembled woods from a fairy tale. It had tall, lush green trees, birds chirping, and squirrels and rabbits running across their path. The sun and sky peeked through high above their heads. The deeper the family ventured into the forest, the less they smelled the salty air, and the more they smelled the earth and Mother Nature. It had a peaceful effect.

Danielle ran slightly ahead of her parents, picking up sticks, leaves, and rocks along the way. Sascha and Devon held hands as they walked but did not say much as they watched Danielle and Bella explore. Michael's phone call left a dark cloud hanging over them.

"Mommy, look," Danielle said as she picked up a sparkly item.

"What is that?" Sascha asked as she kneeled down next to her daughter to observe the contents of her tiny hands.

Sascha's brows furrowed as she wiped dirt and leaves from the familiar piece in her hand.

"Look familiar?" Sascha asked as she turned and raised the item up in her hand for her husband to view.

"Yeah, looks just like the mask we found in the cave in New Zealand," Devon said, taking it from her hand to study it.

"What are the odds?" Sascha asked, although they both knew the answer to the question.

"Zero as far as I am concerned."

Dinner that night felt off. Conversation and time together for Devon and Sascha was always easy and effortless, but on this night there was tension in the air and an element of stress and worry hanging over both of them. When they retired to the library after dinner, and after putting Danielle to bed for the night, neither felt like doing much talking. Instead of talking they decided to listen to music and play a game of chess. After an hour of a competitive match, they stood up to head upstairs to bed.

Despite her fatigue Sascha desired her husband and wanted to be close to him. As she snuggled up to Devon in bed, it was not long before he flipped her onto her back and made love to her. Devon's lovemaking was sweet and slow and brought her body to a frenzy multiple times as she spasmed in ecstasy. As her husband kissed her gently and wished her good night, she fell into a deep sleep, only to be awaken a few hours later by her phone vibrating on her nightstand.

Sascha picked up her phone and saw it was a call from her father. Sascha's first thought was to not answer it as it was likely Michael again, playing his mind games. But then she thought better of it, worried it might actually be her dad and there was an emergency. With a pit in her stomach, she answered the phone.

"Hello," Sascha said reluctantly.

"Sascha, there's been a terrible accident," her father said frantically on the other end of the line.

As Sascha told her father she was on her way, a groggy Devon sat up and asked her what was going on.

"There's been an accident. Maggie ran her car into a tree and is in critical condition. We need to go now," Sascha said, and she started crying. "I did this. This is all my fault."

"What? Let's not jump to conclusions. This is not your fault, and we don't know that Michael had anything to do with this."

"Yes, we do. He warned me to stop looking for him, and I didn't. He did this."

CHAPTER 25

Sascha tapped her fingers against the armrest as they drove up the coast to Sparkle Bay, a northern Californian seaside town full of beaches, bluffs, and beautiful views wherever you turned. It was the picturesque, quaint town where Sascha and Sabrina had grown up.

It felt like they had been driving forever, but it had really only been two hours. Sabrina, James, and Drew slept in the back seat while Devon drove the large SUV as Sascha fidgeted anxiously in the passenger seat. Danielle had been left at home in the care of Lena and Tatum, with Tom and Matt for protection.

Sascha was unsure of Maggie's condition, but if she made it through this, Sascha wanted Maggie and her father to come stay with them while she recovered and until Michael was caught. Sascha knew he was behind whatever happened to Maggie and feared matters would only get worse for her loved ones the longer he was on the run.

It was afternoon when Sascha, Devon, and Sabrina all arrived at the busy but small three-story hospital. After waiting a few minutes at the front desk to be directed to the intensive care unit, the group found their father pacing in the waiting room. The sight of her father broke Sascha's heart.

"What happened, Dad? Is Maggie all right?" Sascha asked as she and Sabrina hugged their weary-looking father.

"As far as the accident, I don't know, and no one seems to be sure what happened. I was initially told she lost control of her car and ran into a tree. The roads were slick, and it was foggy out last night, so it is possible. But now the police are saying there were no skid marks or any evidence that she tried to apply her brakes before the accident. I don't know. Maybe she fell asleep or had a heart attack for all they know," her father choked out, and he sat down in a waiting room chair and put his face in his hands and sobbed.

"Oh, Dad," a teary Sabrina said, sitting next to her father.

Sascha and Devon made eye contact with one another but said nothing, and although she believed deep down this was the handiwork of Michael, she did not need to upset her father any more than he already was. When the time was right, she would share her suspicions with him and the police.

"Has anyone called Christian?" Sabrina asked.

"Yes. I called him when they took her into surgery, and he's on his way now," John said.

"I cannot believe this is happening," Sascha stated, and she, too, started pacing.

"John, did they say what type of injury she has?" Devon asked.

"It's pretty bad, son. She has a broken pelvis, a collapsed lung, and swelling on the brain," he responded as tears continued to fall down his face.

Sabrina hugged and consoled her father, while Devon and Sascha went in search of a doctor or nurse to get an update on Maggie's surgery, which had been going on for four hours already. A kind nurse assisted them and said she would have someone from the surgical team come out and provide an update shortly. Twenty minutes later the surgeon came out to the waiting room and spoke with the family. A focused and serious Christian arrived just in time for the briefing.

"The surgery went well," the surgeon started. "We were able to repair all injuries, including reducing the swelling of the brain, but we will need to wait until she wakes up to determine if there is any permanent damage. We will be keeping her in a medically induced coma for the next twenty-four hours to give her body additional time to heal. With the seriousness of her injuries, coupled with her advanced age, the next few hours will be critical."

"Are you saying she could die?" Christian asked almost in a whisper.

"What I am saying is that we will need to be patient and wait and see. It's going to be a long night. Once she comes out of surgery, you can see her for a short while, and of course, Mr. Olivier, you may stay with her, but it would be best for the rest of you to go home for the night and return in the morning. I can assure you we will call if anything changes with your mother's medical status."

Sascha pulled Christian into a hug as he began to cry. "She's going to be all right. I know it," she quietly said to him, wanting to believe her own words. Christian nodded and gave Sascha a tight squeeze, then quickly gathered himself, pulled away from her hug, and once again had a serious, emotionless expression in place.

An hour later the family was notified Maggie was in her intensive care unit room, and they could go back for a brief time. Sascha was unprepared for what she saw. Gasping at the sight of Maggie, tears were once again brought to all of their eyes. Maggie's head was bandaged, her pelvis was in a cast, and she was battered and bruised all over.

"I know it looks bad, but black eyes and a swollen face are

very common with car accidents and head injuries," the surgeon said as he walked into the room after them. "She had no major facial injuries aside from a broken nose, and the swelling will go down quickly, but you should expect the bruising to last for some time. She is going to need physical therapy for her hip and pelvis injuries, and while we are keeping her in the medically induced coma, her scans look normal, and her prognosis is good."

The doctor's words brought a little relief to Sascha. With the exception of Sascha's father, the group departed for her childhood home for the night, with Devon stating he would be back shortly with an overnight bag for his father-in-law.

Morning came quickly for Sascha and the family as they had hardly slept the night before, and all had been exhausted. Putting on a pot of coffee, Sascha started making breakfast. Visiting hours were still a few hours away, and they all needed to eat something after the emotionally draining previous day they all had. At breakfast Sascha would break the news to Sabrina and Christian about Michael's threat and how Maggie may have been his latest victim. She would not blame Christian if he were angry with her or faulted her for all of this, but he deserved to know everything. After all she had a choice, and she could have stopped hunting Michael after his warning, but she ignored it, and now Maggie had paid the price.

Devon was the first one to come out and join Sascha that morning. He looked exhausted.

"How did you sleep last night?" Sascha asked her sleepy-eyed husband.

"Terrible," he said as she planted a kiss on his cheek. "You know, ever since I met you, I have always wished that we had met sooner. Maybe met when we were teens or something. Me sneaking into your bedroom window and making out and having our first time together, but my God, that horribly uncomfortable bed ruins the fantasy." As Devon chuckled, sipping his coffee, Sascha handed him a plate with bacon, eggs, and toast. Thanking his wife, Devon dug in to his food.

"Morning."

Sascha looked up to find Christian standing in the kitchen doorway.

"Good morning, Christian. Please, come in and sit down, and I'll make you a plate," Sascha said, and she prepared Christian's plate and poured him a cup of coffee.

Christian sat quietly, sipping his coffee and eating. The silence was uncomfortable for several reasons, and while Devon seemed perfectly content to let the awkward silence continue, Sascha could not bear it.

"Is Yvonne going to make it in today?" Sascha questioned, wondering where Christian's new bride was at.

"No," Christian said without further explanation. He gave her an odd stare and then went back to eating his toast.

Sascha took the hint and dropped the subject of Yvonne for the moment, but she planned on finding out why Yvonne was not present. Yvonne adored Maggie, so it made no sense that she would choose not to come unless Christian told her not to.

"Hey, Devon, you know, I just remembered, we had all those security cameras installed around the house last year for my parents. Have you watched the camera footage yet?"

"No, but I'm on it," he responded, pulling out his cell phone. "When do we think it happened?"

"Two nights ago," Sascha stated.

"Wait, what's going on here? What happened two nights ago?" Christian asked as he stared at the pair.

"I think Michael Ghant is behind your mother's car accident."

"How so, and why would he want to hurt my mother? She is the kindest, most generous person I know."

"The how would be having someone tamper with her car's brakes, and the motivation would be to punish me for not doing as he said," Sascha replied, unable to make eye contact with Christian.

"Because you're still searching for him?" Christian asked angrily.

"Yes, and I am so sorry. He warned me that if we continued to hunt him, there would be a price to pay, and I didn't heed his warning. I never in a million years would want to see Maggie hurt."

"This is not your fault. I don't blame you, and I know my mother wouldn't either," Christian responded as he stared off into the distance.

"Thank you for that," Sascha said, reaching across the small table to cover his hand with hers. When Christian's eyes locked with hers, she saw love in his eyes and quickly pulled her hand back.

"I think I found the culprit," Devon informed them, looking up from his phone. "Do either of you recognize this person?"

Devon held the phone out for Sascha and Christian to view. Christian immediately said he did not recognize the person, but as Sascha looked at the phone, she gasped and zoomed in closer on the face of the figure in the video and recognized the person.

"Yes!" Sascha responded, taking the phone from her husband's hand to examine the video closer.

"Well, who is it?" both Devon and Christian asked in unison.

"It's Mona Castillo."

CHAPTER 26

"Who's Mona Castillo?" Christian asked.

"Mona Castillo?" Sabrina exclaimed as she entered the kitchen.

Sascha paused as she bit her lip and looked around the room and thought about how to explain who Mona Castillo was. Sascha had only met Mona once, but she had left a lasting impression on her. Mona Castillo was a warden at the prison where Gina Campbell had been held, and the morning Sascha went to visit Gina, Warden Castillo had personally informed Sascha of the prisoner's untimely death by suicide. Sascha never believed Gina killed herself, although the warden had been adamant of it being otherwise.

Although Mona Castillo seemed suspicious and gave Sascha the creeps, she had no evidence to pinpoint any wrongdoing on the warden's part. Sascha had all but forgotten about Mona Castillo until a suspicious woman, matching Mona's description, was found tampering with Cate's medications in her rehabilitation facility. With her large, six-foot frame, long dark hair, and the distinct scar on her chin, Mona Castillo was not very conspicuous. Sascha quickly put two and two together and realized Mona was likely one of Michael's henchmen, and after Maggie's most recent accident, she was clearly still on his payroll and up to no good again.

Unfortunately for Mona, Michael rarely left witnesses or his accomplices alive. If she was on his payroll and doing his dirty work, then it was only a matter of time before her dead body was found somewhere too. *Foolish woman,* Sascha thought, but she did not feel sorry for her. Not one bit. After sharing Mona Castillo's history with the group, they sat in silence for a few moments until Christian looked at Sascha.

"I have to ask, and I swear I am not judging you or blaming you, and God knows how easy it is to fall in love with you and obsess over you—"

"But?" Devon interrupted Christian, clearly annoyed by the words.

"But," Christian continued, after giving Devon an annoyed glance, "this Michael Ghant is without a doubt a diabolical man, and you have known him since childhood. How did you never see any of this over the years?"

Sascha sat quietly for a moment. She did not feel attacked by Christian's questions, but she did feel like everyone was secretly judging her for bringing a psychopath into their lives.

"That's a fair question, and I get it. I have known Michael for nearly thirty years, and during that time I have never even seen him angry, not until his marriage to Cate. He hid his dark side from me for years, and he hid it well. That's the thing about people like him. He wears many masks. He is cunning, manipulative, and devious," Sascha said, and she got herself a glass of water.

"Sascha is right," Sabrina chimed in. "I have known Michael for years too, and up until two years ago, I would have sworn he was one of the nicest, kindest men I knew. He fooled everyone around him, not just Sascha. Besides, Christian, are you really that great of a judge of character?"

Sascha gasped at Sabrina's words, which were more of a statement than a question. Cate's bluntness seemed to be rubbing off on her, and Sascha was not sure she could take both of them being like that. Sascha searched Christian's face for a reaction, but all he did was chuckle and went back to eating his breakfast. Sascha wanted to ask about Yvonne but now did not seem like the appropriate time, so she asked about politics instead.

As Sascha and Christian continued to speak about his transition from district attorney to United States congressman and how that was going, Devon stepped away for a call, and Sabrina made herself a plate and quietly listened to the discussion. Devon returned moments later, stating he had sent the video of Mona Castillo to the local police department, and they were looking into the matter and considered Mona Castillo a person of interest. Mona was dumb enough to be caught on camera, which probably meant it was time for Michael to dispose of her. Sascha did not expect Mona Castillo to be found alive.

A short while later, it was time for the group to return to the hospital, and as everyone started to leave the kitchen to get ready, Sascha asked Christian to stay back for a discussion.

Before Sascha could speak, Christian quickly said, "I hope you don't think I was victim blaming because that is not what I meant. I apologize if it came off that way."

"Thank you but no worries. I did not take it that way, and I can tell you that I constantly go over my interactions with Michael from previous years, trying to find the signs I missed, and they are not there. But that's not what I wanted to speak with you about."

"Oh, okay. What's up?" Christian said with a look of relief.

"I hate to even bring this up, especially now, and I'm not sure if there is any truth to it, but I thought you needed to know I was told Yvonne previously dated Michael."

Christian's eyes met Sascha's, but his face was expressionless. *Goodness, he has the best poker face ever*, Sascha thought.

"I recently found out that information as well," he said coolly.

"So it's true then? Is that why Yvonne is not here?"

"It's true, and the reason she did not come is because she is having bad morning sickness."

"Oh, she's pregnant. Congrat—" Sascha started.

"But if she had been here when I found out Michael was behind my mother nearly being killed, I don't think I could have tolerated her presence."

Sascha resisted the urge to point out the unfairness that Yvonne was being penalized for dating Michael briefly, while Michael's motivation for wreaking havoc on everyone's life was because of his obsession with Sascha.

"I know what you're thinking, but she lied to me and has been deceptive from the very beginning of our relationship. I have always been honest with her, and while I knew this would not be a marriage like, well, yours, I thought we could have a friendship and a partnership."

"What are you saying?"

"I'm saying a baby bought her some time, but I do not want to be with a woman I cannot trust."

"Trust? Quite the double standard there, Christian. Aren't you in love with someone else?" Sascha asked, annoyed with the irony of his words.

"Like I said, I have been honest with her from the beginning. She knew where my heart lay, and she made a choice. My feelings are not going to change."

"It just sounds so harsh," Sascha said, and she felt sorry for pregnant Yvonne.

"Yeah, well, betrayal is harsh as well," Christian stated, and he stood up and walked away.

Ugh, Sascha knew she needed to stay out of Christian and Yvonne's marriage, but she wanted to help fix it somehow. But maybe that was not something she could fix. A frustrated Sascha marched off to her room to get changed for the hospital.

Twenty minutes later the group was on their way back to the hospital to check in on Maggie and their father. Arriving to the hospital, they found a doctor removing a tube from Maggie's throat and a groggy Maggie slowly returning to them. While John held one of Maggie's hands, Christian walked over and took his mother's other hand in his hand as he started to tear up. Sabrina walked over and put her arm around Christian, offering him emotional support.

"Where are Sascha and Devon?" Maggie asked with a hoarse voice.

"We're here," Sascha responded as she and Devon walked around the bed to where her father stood and put supportive hands on Maggie's arm.

"My beautiful family," Maggie said slowly as she looked around the room.

"Yea! You're awake," a voice said from the doorway, and the group turned to find Yvonne standing there with a large bouquet of flowers.

Sascha walked over to Yvonne, told her to come in, and took the bouquet from her to place on a table beside Maggie's bed.

As Yvonne entered the room, the mood changed. Maggie and John were warm and kind to Yvonne, but Christian was cold toward his wife, and his eyes showed his fury. Yvonne, seemingly oblivious to her husband's ire, turned to him and asked, "Honey, did you already share our good news?"

Sabrina's eyes got big as she looked to Sascha expectantly. Sascha gave a slight nod of her head because she knew her sister was guessing the news was Yvonne's pregnancy.

Christian looked pained and then put a small smile on his face and announced he was going to be a father. Maggie yelped as best she could while Devon and John congratulated Christian.

Sascha hugged Yvonne and asked her how she was feeling, to which Yvonne said she was struggling with awful morning sickness and said she was sick the entire flight and drive out there.

"Oh no, I'm so sorry to hear that. There are a few tips I can share with you that may help with your morning sickness," Sascha said as Yvonne moved to her husband's side in an attempt to appear as a united couple. Casually moving away from her touch, Christian was having none of it.

As Sascha observed them, she got the impression that something else was going on, and Christian had every right to be angry with Yvonne, but for now she just wanted to support the mother-to-be.

"About how far along are you?" Sascha asked, trying to cut the tension in the room.

"Well, we had our first appointment last week, and we're almost seven weeks along then. Which makes us officially eight weeks pregnant," Yvonne shared excitedly.

"Isn't it bad luck to share pregnancy news in the first three months?" Sabrina asked, looking to Yvonne.

Yvonne appeared to be flustered by the question. Before Yvonne could answer, Sascha chimed in, "No, it's not considered bad luck. Many couples just choose not to share their news until they are past the twelve-week mark, but I'm sure this baby is perfectly healthy, and everything will be fine."

"Yes, our baby boy is perfection," Yvonne said, rubbing her nonexistent baby bump.

The room was quiet as the tension was nearly palpable for everyone, except Yvonne, who seemed incapable of reading the room.

Sascha watched her father and Christian make eye contact before her father asked everyone to leave the room to allow Maggie to get some rest. The group said their good-byes to the patient and quickly exited the room, but the tension followed them. Christian excused himself and Yvonne while they went off to speak privately.

"Someone's in trouble," Sabrina said as she watched the couple walk down the hall.

Devon excused himself to take a work call, while the sisters speculated on the family drama.

"What do you think is going to happen with those two?" Sabrina asked.

"I don't know, but I'm thinking nothing good. He's pretty pissed, and Christian doesn't strike me as a forgiving man or someone big on second chances."

"I almost feel sorry for Yvonne. Almost," Sabrina said, shaking her head. "I mean, Christian is hot and all, and successful, but I would never marry a man in love with another woman, especially if that woman is his stepsister and someone who is going to always be in his life. Foolish."

"I'm no bigger fan of Yvonne than you are, and yes, it was foolish to marry a man whose affections lie elsewhere, but love makes us do stupid things. And I don't blame her for fighting for the man she loves," Sascha stated before being shushed by Sabrina as the couple returned.

Sascha looked from Christian to Yvonne but neither spoke. Christian stood tall and rigid, his brown eyes dark with anger. Yvonne, in contrast, was slouched in defeat, with red-rimmed eyes from crying. Devon returned to the group moments later and asked what the plan was. Sascha suggested heading back to the house and ordering in food for dinner. Everyone nodded in silence and walked out to the parking lot. Christian and Yvonne drove separately in her rental car, and although Sascha hated to admit it, she was happy to not have to be around their tension and sadness, even if only for a short car ride.

By the time they all arrived back at the house, Yvonne had her happy face back on again, which only made Sascha feel sadder for her and furious with Christian for being cold and cruel to his wife. The group planned to spend that night exploring Sparkle Bay and enjoying dinner together before splitting up the following day. Devon, Sascha, and Yvonne were all returning home the following day, while Sabrina and Christian were staying for the week.

Sascha needed to get everything in order for her father and Maggie to come live with them while Maggie recovered. A home health aide would be needed, as well as a physical therapist to attend to Maggie. It was going to be a long road to recovery, and she was going to need help and family around her, and Sascha knew her aging father could not do it alone.

After dinner, Sascha and Devon took a walk out to the cliffs. It was a full moon, and the light made the ocean water glisten and sparkle for as far as the eye could see. Sascha leaned back on Devon as he wrapped his arms around her, and they enjoyed the sound of the waves hitting against the rocks below.

"I love you," Devon whispered, and he kissed his wife's cheek. Sascha smiled to herself. Her husband's touch still gave her butterflies in her stomach.

CHAPTER 27

*S*ascha woke up feeling tired with sore breasts and the ability to smell everything. She smelled the damp, salty air seeping in from a partially open window in her room. Sascha smelled the bergamot, cardamon, and musk from Devon's shower gel he would have used earlier while she was still sleeping. She could even smell the wild roses from her garden below.

As she lay in bed, a smile covered her face in happiness. *Duh,* she thought to herself, *I'm pregnant.* Doctors told her she would not be able to have any children after the car accident caused by Gina Campbell, which seriously injured Sascha and caused a miscarriage. Thankfully, a child-free life was not her fate and along came Danielle, whom both she and Devon considered a gift, and they treasured her, but they did not expect to be as fortunate a second time.

Sascha's monthly flow had always been irregular, but if she had to guess, she was nearly four months along. She called her doctor who had an appointment available for that morning. Sascha hurried and got ready and went into Devon's office to let him know she would be back shortly.

"Oh, where are you off to this early?" he asked, looking up from the multiple computer screens on his desk.

"I have a doctor's appointment," Sascha responded, reluctant to share the news in case she was wrong.

"Are you not feeling well?" he asked, standing up and walking over to her, putting the back of his hand to her forehead.

Looking around she noticed Delilah was not present. She would not want to risk Michael finding out about her pregnancy. "Where is your assistant?"

"She has not shown up the past two days," Devon said with a pondering expression on his face.

"Do we think she figured out we were on to her, or has she been disposed of by her evil employer?"

"Well, if we know Michael, both statements are probably true, and she is no longer alive."

"Oh my god. I hope that's not the case. Should we report her missing?"

"I already have Matt looking into it. She hasn't been seen since we went up to Sparkle Bay. Now enough about her and back to my question," Devon said, focusing on Sascha intensely.

"No, I'm not sick," Sascha said with a tentative smile. "I think I'm pregnant."

"Really?"

"Well, I'm pretty sure, but of course I want to get confirmation from the doctor before—"

"Yes!" Devon cheered, picking her up and twirling her around in his arms.

"Don't get too excited just yet," Sascha said as Devon put her down. "Do you want to come to my appointment this morning? I know you are—"

"Yes, let's go," Devon said, grabbing his blazer.

Once arriving at the doctor's office, Sascha became

nervous thinking she could be wrong about her pregnancy and that she was getting her hopes, and Devon's, up for nothing. Before the doctor came to see her, she had her blood drawn and had to pee on a stick. By the time the doctor called them back, she was squeezing Devon's hand.

"All right, let's get a look at that baby," the doctor said as she followed them into the room.

"Wait. So I am pregnant?" Sascha asked expectantly.

"Yes, you are and pretty far along based on your hormone levels." The doctor directed Sascha to lie back, and she squeezed gel onto her stomach and began an ultrasound. As Sascha heard the thumping of her baby's heart, her eyes teared up, and as she looked to Devon, she saw his eyes fill with tears as well.

"All right, just going to take a few measurements, but based on the size, you look to be around fifteen, possibly sixteen or seventeen weeks."

"And the baby looks healthy? No problems?" Sascha asked anxiously.

"Baby looks healthy. Now of course we will run more tests throughout the stages of your pregnancy, and you are a little older than you were the last time you were pregnant, but you are healthy, in great shape, and everything appears perfectly normal."

Sascha breathed a sigh of relief.

The doctor stared at her and asked, "Is there a particular concern you have?"

"Well, I have just been under a lot of stress, and I was worried that it might have affected the baby."

"Significant stress can affect the mother's health and in turn affect the baby. I want to suggest you maintain your routine, start taking your prenatal vitamins, keep exercising, writing, and running but reduce anything in your life that's causing you stress. Got it?"

"Got it," Sascha responded as she and Devon made eye contact. "Should I be worried that I don't even have a baby bump at four months pregnant?"

"No. Just the added benefit of being in great shape, but trust me, that baby will make sure you know they are there. Now do you want to know the gender? The blood test has the results," the doctor asked, looking to the couple.

As the couple made eye contact with one another, they each shook their head no.

～

"CAN you believe Danielle is going to be a big sister?" Devon asked as they arrived home.

"No, but how excited are you?" Sascha responded, smiling joyously.

"I'm over the moon. I was already the luckiest man in the world with my two girls, and now we get to grow our family."

A rarely emotional Devon pulled Sascha into a long embrace. Pulling away, eyes once again misty, Devon said he needed to get back to work. Before going back into his office to work, he suggested a celebratory dinner that evening. Sascha readily agreed and knew she needed to get back to work as well and get some writing done, but she was far too excited to sit still and concentrate. With her mind going a hundred miles a minute, Sascha decided to go for a walk and make plans for a small dinner party with her family to announce her pregnancy.

Sascha changed into her running clothes and stepped outside and realized she needed to grab a sweatshirt as it was chillier than expected. Turning around she found Matt standing behind her, clearly planning to follow.

"Matt, I'm not leaving the Swell. There's no reason to accompany me."

Matt stood in place by the door and simply said, "Marissa Tanner."

Sascha nodded her head in understanding as she went to the coat closet for a hoodie. If Anna was not the culprit, and Sascha firmly believed in Anna's innocence, then that meant someone else was behind the gates of the Swell or someone with access to their neighborhood was a killer, and therefore everyone was a suspect and not to be trusted.

As Sascha left the house, she popped in her earbuds and began a brisk walk. As she walked through the neighborhood, she passed Marissa Tanner's home. Sascha stopped for a brief moment and stared at the grand, brick home, wondering what really happened there on the night of Marissa's death. Sascha noticed a familiar car parked in the driveway of the home and recognized it as belonging to one of the detectives who had interviewed her. They were back, but hopefully the detectives did not need to interview her or her household again.

As she turned to walked away, Sascha was surprised to see Anna walking toward her.

"Should you be over here?" Sascha asked, and she ushered her friend away.

"Probably not but I have so many questions and cannot believe this is really happening to me."

Sascha invited Anna back to her house to talk. It was too cold to continue out in the damp air. Arriving back at her home, Sascha offered Anna a cup of coffee, while she had a glass of orange juice. Anna gave her an odd look but said nothing.

"What is your lawyer saying?"

"Nothing good. We were hoping the district attorney

would drop the charges, but it doesn't seem like that is going to happen." Anna put her face in her hands and began to cry.

Sascha comforted her friend with a hug but had no idea what to say to her. *What does one say to someone being falsely accused of murder?* she thought.

"Devon and I are here for you. Do you know if there are any other suspects?"

Anna shook her head.

"Well, I think you need to get a good private detective on this," Sascha encouraged.

"I know, and I will get one," Anna said, then paused. "I am going to sell the house."

"What? Why?" Sascha asked in surprise.

"My defense is going to cost a small fortune, and the upkeep and fees to live here in the Swell is just too much."

"I told you Devon and I would take care of your legal fees."

"And I am so grateful and appreciative of the offer, but I cannot let you do that. Besides, after it is all said and done, me and the girls will need a new start, and I don't think we could have that if we continue to live here."

"I understand," Sascha said, and she hugged her friend again. "Oh, I'm going to miss you."

"We will still be friends, and if I'm not in prison, we will still hang out."

Looking at her watch, Anna stood up. "I had better get going. There are a couple of showings this afternoon, and me and the girls cannot be there."

"You're doing showings already?"

Sadly nodding her head, Anna departed.

CHAPTER 28

Life had been quiet and simple for a few weeks at the Montague residence, that was until Devon received a call from the police regarding a body found floating in the bay. The police asked him to come in to identify the body and to answer some questions.

"This makes no sense. Why would they think you know this person?" Sascha asked nervously.

"No idea, but there's only one way to find out. Are you coming?" Devon asked Sascha as he grabbed his jacket and waited for her to grab hers.

"Absolutely," Sascha responded. There was no way she was going to sit home on pins and needles waiting to find out who this mystery dead person was and what their link was to Devon.

An hour later Sascha and Devon met two detectives at the morgue. She had never been to a morgue before and felt both sad and creeped out to be there. Walking in she immediately recognized Detective Martinez from the investigation of her break-in and stalker case and felt a little better being there with someone she was familiar with.

Sascha was quickly reminded that Detective Martinez always kept a cool, calm demeanor, and he had an air of confidence about him. He was attractive but not overly appealing with a medium build, hazel eyes, and wavy black hair. He made eye contact with Sascha but did not say a word and held her gaze until Devon spoke.

"I'd like to see the body now," Devon said in a commanding tone.

"Follow me," the detective said, and walked them down the hall to stand in front of a large window.

Detective Martinez pressed a buzzer and spoke into an intercom, stating, "We're ready for Jane Doe." Moments later a sheet-covered body was wheeled on a gurney into Devon's and Sascha's view. Detective Martinez looked to Sascha, who nodded her head as Devon laced his fingers with hers and braced herself for the viewing. When the sheet was pulled back to uncover the body to the shoulders, Sascha gasped as she recognized the once-beautiful face of Delilah Cahill.

"Do you recognize this woman?" the detective asked.

"Yes. It's Delilah Cahill," Devon responded, clearly shaken. "Up until a few weeks ago, she had been my personal assistant."

Speaking into the intercom again, Detective Martinez said, "We're good," and the face of Delilah Cahill was covered again and wheeled away.

Turning to Devon, the detective asked, "And why did she stop working for you?"

"Because she was up to no good," Devon responded coolly. "She was a plant or a spy of some sort. Maybe she worked for a business competitor or a disgruntled ex-employee or maybe even Michael Ghant. Whoever sent her in sent her to spy and to cause marital issues."

"And did it work?" Detective Martinez asked with expectant eyes.

"What do you think?" Devon responded, pulling Sascha in closer to him.

"When was the last time you saw her?" Detective Martinez questioned.

"It was on the fourteenth, about three weeks ago," Devon responded.

"And how was she when you last saw her?"

"I don't know. I suppose she was behaving odd, sort of cagey. I think she suspected we were on to her, and she was about to be let go," Devon said, and he appeared to be trying to remember the event.

"So you never actually fired her?" Detective Martinez asked with suspicion in his voice.

"No. I never had a chance to because she just stopped showing up to work. I assumed she knew it was coming."

"A woman who works for you goes missing and you just do nothing?"

"We filed a missing person's report, and I have had my security team going by to her last known address to see if she shows up. It is you, Detective, and your pals who have done nothing," Devon coldly stated.

Silence ensued as Devon and Detective Martinez glared at one another.

"I have a question," Sascha said, breaking the tension. "If she was a Jane Doe and you did not know who she was, how did you know to contact Devon about her?"

The detective pulled out his phone and showed Sascha and Devon a picture of a leather luggage tag that was embroidered with Devon's name.

"This was found shoved down the victim's throat," Detective Martinez said in a disgusted voice.

This time both Devon and Sascha gasped at the horror of the information just shared. Devon pulled Sascha into his arms to comfort her, only for her to quickly pull back after having a realization.

"Montenegro!" Sascha exclaimed.

"Michael?" Devon questioned.

"Yes. He had to take it from your bag when he was in our hotel room in Montenegro," Sascha said, while shaking her head in disbelief.

"I'm not following," Detective Martinez chimed in.

"We've been hunting Michael Ghant for almost a year and nearly had him in Montenegro, but someone tipped him off. He got away but not before raiding our things in our hotel room," Devon said in disgust.

"Which is where you think he took the luggage tag?" the detective asked.

"It has to be. Devon just started traveling with that particular luggage set. It was a recent gift from me," Sascha said.

Detective Martinez nodded his head, took notes, asked a few more questions, and after another ten minutes of discussion, told them they were free to go. Devon and Sascha returned home in silence as they both tried to process the most recent events. That night Sascha tossed and turned all night and could not stop thinking about Delilah's face and the dark marks on her neck, clearly indicating she was strangled to death.

A FEW DAYS LATER, Devon knocked on Sascha's office door and entered carrying papers. Looking up from her computer, Sascha said, "What's that?"

"It's the report on Delilah Cahill, or should I say Tatiana Petrov."

"Who?" Sascha said as she snatched the papers from

Devon's hands. Quickly reading through the papers, minutes later she set the documents down on her desk and leaned back in her chair in shock.

"So does a Delilah Cahill even exist? A Delilah Cahill who worked with Emma?" Sascha asked, trying to stop herself from firing off more questions to Devon.

"Oh yes, Delilah Cahill exists, and she did work with Emma too. But that Delilah has been missing for eight months."

"Oh my god. Michael strikes again," Sascha said, rubbing her temples as her head started to pound.

"Sweetheart, please do not get yourself worked up. Michael knows his days are numbered and that we are closing in on him," Devon said in a calming tone.

"Devon, this is crazy. The bodies are piling up, and it still feels like we are no closer to capturing Michael. Who else has to die for this man's obsession?"

"Sascha, Michael's murderous behavior is not your fault," Devon said as he walked around the desk to pull his wife into his arms.

"You say that, but it is kind of my fault. If only I had seen who he really was years ago, none of this would be happening now."

"I don't agree," Devon said, pulling back from their embrace and staring into her eyes. "And I'm not going to stand here in front of my strong, beautiful, intelligent wife and listen to her blame herself for some grown man's actions," Devon stated firmly.

Sascha stood there quietly, thinking for a moment before telling Devon he was right.

"I know I am." He chuckled. "But now what? Where do we go from here?" he asked, once again serious.

"I think we go back to London."

"Why?"

"Because I don't think Emma's death, the letter she left you, and the real Delilah Cahill missing are all a coincidence that so happened to put Tatiana Petrov into our lives. I think it was evil at work and Michael playing the long game."

CHAPTER 29

$\mathcal{S}$ascha was distressed during their entire flight to London. She had to sit with the possibility that Michael had killed Emma too, and if that were true, how did she and Devon break the news to Emma's children? Turning to her husband, who was working on his laptop, she let out a sigh. He immediately closed the computer and asked her if she wanted to talk about it.

"What are we going to tell Emma's children?" Sascha asked, tasting blood as she bit her lip.

"We don't need to tell them anything just yet because we don't actually know anything. Emma had been sick for a while, and she was going to die sooner rather than later. That much we do know."

"True, but her death was likely hastened by Michael or one of his minions. If you remember, she had been getting better and suddenly took a turn for the worse and died. And then to conveniently have those letters in her hospital room and not her home office? It's all just too weird and too much of a coincidence to not be foul play," Sascha responded with certainty.

"You're right. It did not occur to me at the time to view her death as suspicious because of her age and her failing health but now…" Devon said, his words trailing off.

"But now what?" Sascha asked, prodding her husband to finish his thoughts.

"Now I realize I let grief cloud my thinking. The timing of the events and the letters should have raised red flags for me as well, but my brain just shut down for a while there, and after that I just focused on you and Danielle and work so I didn't have to think about Emma's death."

Sascha nodded, took her husband's hand, and laid her head on Devon's shoulder. "You know what we need to do, right?"

"Yes," Devon responded in a soft voice. "We have to let Emma's children know everything because we are going to need their permission to have her body exhumed for testing."

Feeling sick Sascha leaned back in her seat and put her hand on her growing belly. She requested a ginger ale, hoping to soothe her queasiness, but she knew her upset stomach had nothing to do with her pregnancy and everything to do with the tasks ahead of them.

Hours later the Montagues arrived to a gloomy London. The weather matched her mood as Sascha was filled with dread at the thought of the conversation they planned that evening with Emma's children. Two of Emma's children, Christopher and Amelia, would be joining them for dinner that evening at the London townhouse, while Henry, the youngest son, would participate via video call as he was currently out of the country. The only way an investigation could be opened into Emma's death and her body exhumed for testing would be if her family agreed. Sascha believed Emma's children would be heartbroken to know their mother may have been murdered, but they deserved the truth and the opportunity to seek justice.

Arriving at the townhouse, Sascha gave directions to house staff in preparation for their dinner that evening, went up to take a shower, and then lay down for a much-needed nap. She was mentally and physically drained and needed to recharge and prepare herself for what she expected to be an emotionally charged evening. Planning to only nap for an hour, Sascha was awakened nearly two hours later by Devon, who informed her their guests would be arriving in an hour.

A groggy Sascha quickly got dressed for the evening, keeping her aesthetic simple and elegant. She dressed in fitted, dark-gray slacks and a black cashmere sweater and pulled her curly hair back into a loose chignon. She applied a light layer of makeup to her glowing skin and wore her favorite pair of diamond stud earrings and her wedding band. Sascha Montague was a stunning beauty without even trying. While standing in front of the mirror adding her final touches, Devon walked up behind Sascha, wrapped his arms around her waist, and placed his hands on her small baby bump.

"You're looking beautiful this evening," Devon said as he pulled her body back into his.

"So are you," Sascha responded, a soft smile on her lips.

The couple made eye contact with one another in the mirror and silently comforted one another. The couple continued their silent communication for a few more moments before there was a knock at the bedroom door. It was the house manager informing Sascha the guests would be arriving in fifteen minutes and requested her approval on the final arrangements for the evening. Sascha quickly kissed her husband before following the house manager downstairs.

The London house staff was a well-trained and experienced group who required little direction once provided with basic information on planned events, and this evening was no different. Sascha gave instructions for dinner that evening to be a simple, family-style meal served with wine and bread. The chef decided to serve shepherd's pie, which coincidentally had been Emma's favorite dish. She had even taught Sascha how to make it a few years back, although hers never tasted as good as Emma's.

Christopher and Amelia arrived together at 7:30 p.m. on the dot. Sascha smiled as she opened the door to greet them, thinking how Emma was always punctual and had clearly taught her children to be the same way. Sascha and Devon were greeted with warm smiles and hugs but could tell the guests were tense with anticipation for the short-notice invite. After a housekeeper took their coats, Sascha invited them to join her and Devon in the library for cocktails before dinner was served. While Sascha sipped on ginger ale, Devon and their guests enjoyed glasses of wine. Once the standard pleasantries were done, Emma's daughter asked if she should now call her younger brother for the video chat. Devon replied yes, and an uncomfortable silence took over the room as they all waited for the brother to pick up the call.

Henry finally answered the call after multiple rings and was informed they were all gathered with the Montagues who had some information to share.

"I'm not quite sure how to say this, but I will not belabor the point," Devon said as he began to pace the library before coming to a stop in front of the roaring fireplace. "We suspect foul play may have led to your mother's death."

"What?" Christopher responded, appearing confused by what he heard.

"Michael Ghant, the billionaire who assaulted me. We believe—" Sascha said, before she was interrupted.

"I knew it," Amelia said, standing up from her chair. All eyes on Amelia, she continued. "Well not about Michael Ghant, but there was something off about her death. I remember the day she died like it was yesterday. She hadn't been doing well, and it was touch and go there for a while, which is why I reached out to you to come and say your goodbyes. But then she seemed to pull through and start getting better. On that particular day, I had taken her fresh flowers for her hospital room. We chatted and joked while I brushed her hair, and when the nurse came in to check on her and replace her IV bag, she said everything looked good. Mom sent me off to get myself something to eat while she napped. When I came back, she was still sleeping, and then she suddenly coded, and they had to intubate her, and she died shortly after. Just like that."

"Hmm, I wonder what was in that IV bag. Had you seen this nurse before?" Sascha asked.

"Actually no, now that you mention it," Amelia responded, and she seemed to start putting the pieces of the puzzle together.

A tap came at the library door, informing the group dinner was ready to be served. Once the group was seated at the dinner table, they began filling their plates and their wine glasses, and they quietly ate and drank, each lost in their own thoughts.

"Hold on," Christopher demanded, breaking the silence. "Why would this Ghant guy want to hurt our mother? Makes no sense."

"The letters," Amelia answered her brother as her face turned red in anger.

"How did you know?" Sascha asked.

"The letters always bothered me. I had been tidying my mother's room daily, and I never saw the letters until the day she died, but I didn't question them at the time because I was in complete shock that I had just lost my mother. And after that it didn't seem to really matter."

"What was in the letters?" Henry asked on the phone.

Devon explained the contents of both letters to the group, and Sascha could tell they were more confused than ever.

"We believe the whole motivation was to put Delilah Cahill into our lives and into our home where she could do harm," Sascha stated softly.

"Wow, there sure is a hell of a lot of collateral damage around you," Christopher said nastily to Sascha.

"I know you're upset; we all are. But this isn't Sascha's fault. Sascha is a victim too," Devon said in her defense, but Sascha shook her head at him, silently pleading with him not to continue.

After a few awkward moments of silence, Amelia said, "Why do I get the feeling there's something else?"

"If we are to get the authorities to open an investigation into your mother's death, her body will need to be exhumed, and your permission would be needed for that," Devon said.

Sascha held her breath, waiting their response. The siblings made eye contact and then nodded their heads in agreement.

CHAPTER 30

Sascha's pinging phone drew her attention from writing. Picking it up in annoyance that her "do not disturb" was not on, she saw a breaking news alert that Anna had been indicted on first-degree murder charges, and her case would be going to trial. Upon seeing the news, Sascha immediately grabbed her phone and texted Anna a message of support. She did not expect a response, but Anna texted back a heart emoji. Sascha's heart broke for her friend. According to the news, there had been convincing evidence against Anna to move forward with a trial. Sascha was stunned but still believed Anna was innocent and being set up.

Needing a distraction Sascha quickly dressed in her exercise clothes and had her morning run on the treadmill. Pregnancy did not stop her fitness routine. In fact she felt better than ever in her second trimester and was full of energy. After her run she took a hot shower and went to check in on Danielle, who was just waking up. Sascha got Danielle dressed and ready and took her downstairs as Bella, Toffee, and Greer followed behind them.

"Good morning, my beautiful girls," Devon said as he looked up from his morning paper in the breakfast room. "No Lena today?"

"No. Yesterday I could tell she was coming down with something, so I gave her a few days off to recover."

Devon nodded and continued to look at his wife before finally saying, "Did you see the news?"

"I did. I'm not shocked because this is clearly where this has been heading the entire time, but I am horrified that this is happening to Anna. I mean what kind of evidence could they possibly have against her?"

"I read the court documents online this morning, and it's not looking good for Anna. They have her DNA on the victim's body."

"What kind of DNA? Anything could have been planted," Sascha responded defensively as she made Danielle's breakfast plate and set it in front of her.

"True, but DNA evidence is a hard one to fight and prove that it got on that woman's body by some other means than being the killer."

"Devon, there is not a doubt in my mind that Anna has been set up. She is the perfect fall guy. She lives in this community, is a single, newly divorced woman. Her ex-husband has fallen from grace and is no longer wealthy or influential. You cannot tell me the snobs of the Swell did not want her gone from here. And Marissa for that matter too. Kill two birds with one stone."

"No argument from me that the collective would like her gone from the community, but I doubt there was a neighborhood meeting on killing Marissa or setting Anna up for it. It was only a matter of time before she would be forced to sell and move from here. The upkeep and community fees are not cheap."

"You're right," Sascha reluctantly agreed.

"I'm sorry. I didn't quite catch that. Can you repeat please?" Devon teased.

Sascha giggled in response as she ate her breakfast.

"What do you want to do today? It's supposed to be a beautiful day," Sascha stated.

"How about we go sailing? We can sail over to Treasure Island and explore with Danielle."

"Oh, I would love that. I will have the chef make lunches and snacks for us, and I'll get everything else ready while you take care of the boat."

"Sounds good. Plan on leaving in two hours."

After Sascha gave the chef instructions, she took Danielle and Bella outside to play and run around for a bit. Sascha was sitting, watching Danielle play, when she heard a large truck and banging. Curious, she walked over to the side gate and peered over it, spotting a moving truck in front of Anna's home. Anna was back in jail and would stay there until she stood trial for murder. Sascha wondered who was moving Anna's things. Calling to Danielle and Bella to come to her, Sascha took Danielle's hand as Bella trotted behind them while they crossed the street to Anna's home.

It was not long before Sascha spotted an older woman who resembled Anna. She looked like she could be her mother, but that could not be right since Anna had said her mother was dead. Walking up to the woman to greet her, the woman immediately pulled Sascha into a hug and thanked her for supporting and helping Anna. She introduced herself as Caroline, Anna's aunt, and revealed she was Anna's mother's identical twin sister. *Ah*, Sascha thought, *so twins run in the family.*

Caroline was warm and friendly, much like Anna. Caroline bent down to engage with Danielle and to pet Bella. She told Sascha she had rented a nice house for her and the twins not far from the Swell and would be staying in San Francisco until Anna's trial was over. Sascha smiled and nodded but feared for the worst for Anna. The deck was stacked against her, but she also wanted to hold out hope that her friend would be found innocent. The women continued to talk as movers came in and out of the home with large pieces of furniture.

After a while Sascha saw Tomas exiting the home, carrying items to his car, and with the sight of him, Caroline's demeanor immediately changed. Her body stiffened, and she rolled her eyes. Caroline hated him, and Sascha could not blame her. He had destroyed his family in more ways than one. Seeing Sascha, Tomas gave her a friendly wave. Sascha waved back and said her farewell to Caroline, who seemed to no longer be in a chatting mood.

Leaving Anna's home Sascha felt so many emotions. She truly believed in Anna's innocence, but she did not trust the system. So many rich and powerful people hated Marissa and may have wanted her dead, but unlike the others, Anna was no longer rich or powerful. Anna was an easy scapegoat.

Walking back into her home, Sascha saw Devon standing in the foyer with a questioning expression on his face.

"Where did you all go off to?"

"Across the street. Anna's family is moving today."

"You're still up for going out on the boat today?"

"Absolutely," Sascha responded, trying to sound more excited than she felt.

"Well then hustle up, buttercup. We leave in half an hour," Devon said, and he pulled her in for a soft kiss.

Sascha was so happy they had decided to go out on the water that day. The weather was beautiful, and the sunshine was just what she needed for a mood boost. Danielle was snug in her life jacket and found her sea legs easily. She giggled and laughed as the wind blew her baby curls, reminding Sascha of her younger self. Sascha grew up sailing and felt just as comfortable on the ocean as she did on the land. After docking at Treasure Island to enjoy their lunch and a walk around the island, Devon pointed out to sea.

"We had better get going back home. Looks like there are dark clouds ahead."

Ugh, Sascha thought. The unintended foreshadowing of Devon's words were not lost on her.

$\mathcal{B}$efore Sascha got further along in her pregnancy, her editor and publisher wanted her to do a small promotional tour for several of the newly released versions of her books and in anticipation of the fifth book of the Coven of Plumvale series being released the following year. Although Devon was not crazy about her taking long flights across the Atlantic while she was pregnant, Sascha argued this would be the best time she would have to travel for work for the better part of a year. Devon could have squashed the whole tour if he wanted to, since he owned the publishing company, but he and Sascha agreed long ago that he would not use his power as the owner of the company as a means to interfere in her writing career.

Devon's melancholy mood did not go unnoticed by Sascha as she said her goodbyes to Danielle, him, and her furbabies. When he held her in a tight embrace, she quietly asked him what was the matter. He told her he had a bad feeling about the trip, but Sascha assured him that he need not worry and that she would see him soon on the island. He nodded his head and said goodbye, but for a moment she thought he might demand she not leave.

The plan was for Sascha and her team to be gone for a little less than a week, and after that she would meet Devon and Danielle at their Orcas Island home. Sascha, Tatum, Matt, and Tom all flew out to London in the family jet early on a Tuesday morning. The week was to be jam-packed with events, starting in London, then on to Berlin, Germany, and ending in Paris, France.

Although Sascha felt a little guilty going to Europe for a book tour, she was also excited and anxious to see and talk to her fans again. The London book tour stop was a huge success. Fans of the books and television series came out in droves and lined the street to get their books signed by Sascha. The next day Sascha hit the London media circuit, appearing on two morning shows, a radio show, and a podcast. It was exhausting, but Sascha was humbled by her success and the reception by her fans.

The following day the group flew out to Berlin. Though not the same crush of people she had at her London event, Sascha did a reading to a full crowd and still ran out of time to sign the books of all the attendees. After the midday signing event, Sascha attended the premiere of her television series in Berlin. Marcus Winters and several of the show's cast members also joined the event. It was a fun premiere, and Sascha was happy to see that Cate had accompanied Marcus.

The couple seemed to be getting serious, and Sascha said so to Cate that night at the after-party. Cate was smitten with Marcus, and Marcus adored Cate, but neither ever wanted to get married again, which was understandable for both of them as they had four divorces between the two of them. Marcus's twelve-year-old daughter had also joined the couple for the premiere, and Sascha was pleasantly surprised to witness Cate's interaction with the young girl.

Walking up to Cate after observing the pair, Sascha said, "Ready to be a stepmom?"

"Oh God, no. I think she's just tolerating me to please her dad," Cate responded as she waved her hand, dismissing Sascha's comment.

"I think it's more than that, but I'll drop it for now," Sascha said. She sensed Marcus and his daughter were sensitive topics for Cate, and Cate was still healing from old wounds.

Cate gave Sascha a sweet smile and pulled her best friend into a hug. The women hung out for the rest of the evening until Sascha called it a night to go back to her hotel and get some rest before an early morning flight out to Paris.

Sascha breathed a sigh of relief as she lay down to sleep that night. The tour had been going smooth so far, and while she put on a brave face for everyone, she had been filled with anxiety prior to coming out on the tour because the last spotting of Michael had been in Europe, and she currently had no idea where he could be. If Michael wanted to find Sascha, he could easily do so. Sascha's tour itinerary was no secret, it was being promoted by a marketing firm and her publisher, and her scheduled meet and greets could be found on her website and the publisher's website.

The last few days of the mini European tour were spent in France. After weeks of not hearing a peep from Michael, Sascha took a sigh a relief as she believed Michael would not attempt to make contact with her here, but her gut told her he was planning something big. For now she chose to just enjoy being a tourist in one of her favorite cities while enjoying her fans and her pregnancy.

The first day in Paris, Sascha had just one interview that morning, and then she was free to enjoy the rest of the day touring the city with Tatum, and of course Matt and Tom. They enjoyed lunch and a visit to the Louvre and ordered room service that evening to give Sascha's slightly swollen feet some much-needed rest.

The following day was jam-packed with events, and on the morning of the third day, the group would be flying back to the States. Sascha got up early after a busy day of interviews, a book signing, and attending a ribbon cutting for a new boutique bookstore that was co-owned by two female fantasy writers who were also represented by Sascha's agent. She was excited to head to the private airport to return home.

Upon arriving at the airport, the group was informed their plane was having mechanical issues. There was a smaller plane available, but the pilot stated a large storm was hitting the Washington State area, and it was currently not safe to fly in. The group started looking into commercial flights, but many had been canceled due to weather issues or were completely booked. Sascha put them all down for standby, and when they arrived at the international airport, she was told she was the only one who could make it onto the flight. The others would need to take the next flight.

Sascha told the group she was going to take the flight, and she would see them all soon. A bewildered Matt stared at her and then pleaded with Sascha to wait for the rest of the group, but she knew what flying by herself and going to Orcas Island alone would mean. It would give Michael the opening he had been waiting for. And while going alone to a remote island would give Michael the chance to take her, it would also give her an opportunity to put an end to all of this. While a furious Matt walked away, making a phone call to Devon, Sascha assumed, a teary-eyed Tatum mouthed, "Good luck" to Sascha as she left to board her plane.

CHAPTER 32

Time seemed to stand still and move at warp speed all simultaneously as Sascha traveled to the Seattle, Washington, airport. A powerful storm was pounding the northern Pacific coast and was expected to only get worse as the evening progressed. Sascha was not even sure that she could make it out to the island from the city once she landed. The waters were likely too choppy, and most ferry services were likely suspended.

There was one boat captain she knew who would likely brave the weather for her to the island, but it was going to cost her a pretty penny. Hopefully she could find him before the possibility of getting to the island on this day was gone. She texted Captain Nyles just before boarding and told him when she would be arriving and checked her phone periodically throughout the flight, hoping for a positive response.

The San Francisco area had suffered heavy storms and rains days earlier. Devon was currently stranded in San Francisco, with many roads closed and major flooding throughout the city. Just as her flight took off, she received a three-word text from Devon that said, "Don't do this."

It wasn't that she wanted to do any of this, but the stars were aligning, and now was the time to lure Michael out and finish this once and for all. Michael had been tracking Sascha for years, and she had no doubt that he knew Devon was stuck in San Francisco and that she was on a flight, alone, and traveling to an isolated island without her security team or anyone else to save her from him.

Sascha tried to sleep on the twelve-hour flight and did manage to doze for a bit here and there, but she was too tense to relax and rest. When the plane finally touched done, Sascha was met with pouring rain. Entering the airport she looked up at the screens and saw all flights were canceled. The worst of the storm was yet to come.

Checking her phone again after she deboarded the plane, Sascha saw dozens of missed texts from Devon, Matt, and one from Captain Nyles that just said yes. Retrieving her bag Sascha took a taxi to the dock where the old local Captain Nyles had agreed to take her out to the island. The taxi warned her that no one in their right mind would be out on the water in this weather and said they would wait for her and take her back to the city once she realized it was a moot point to try to get out to the island. Exiting the taxi Sascha saw Captain Nyles wave her down to the pier to where his boat was, and she turned and gave the taxi driver the thumbs-up to depart.

Seeing her arrive alone, the captain asked where everyone else was, and she informed him they would all be along shortly.

"I don't think they will. Not in this weather," he replied.

"It's fine. They will get here when they get here," Sascha responded, trying to downplay his look of concern.

"I really don't think you should be going out there alone like this, miss. Most of the island residents have already left. You will be out there all by yourself."

"I know," Sascha stated firmly. "Are we ready to go?"

"Yes, ma'am."

Captain Nyles took Sascha across to the island in a large fishing boat. Sascha had been on the water most of her life, but even she felt seasick in the choppy waters. She took deep breaths to calm her nerves and her stomach and repeated the mantra "you can do this" over and over in her head.

Sascha closed her eyes and saw Michael's smug face, which angered her, but then she gave herself a reminder. Michael thought he would have the element of surprise, but it was really Sascha who would be lying in wait. Sascha slowly felt calmer at that thought.

CHAPTER 33

$\mathcal{A}$s the boat approached the island, and she saw her home up ahead, she started to question her decision to try to lure Michael out into the open. She was pregnant and had a small child at home. *This is madness*, she thought, but there was no turning back now.

The captain pulled his fishing boat directly up to the boat dock on the Montague property. He helped her off the boat and grabbed her bag and said, "I could stay here with you until your husband or friends get here. So you're not out here by yourself. It's not safe."

Sascha recognized the fatherly concern in his face, but him staying meant he would be in danger as well, and she could not allow that.

"I appreciate your concern, and I thank you for bringing me out here, but I'm good. You have a safe trip back and a good night," Sascha responded, ending the conversation.

"Listen, there is a small island security team that is still here. Give them a call if anything happens."

Sascha thanked Captain Nyles, but his words did not sit well with her. The captain wished Sascha a safe evening, got back on his boat, and departed. Sascha lugged her bag up to the house in the pouring, icy rain as the wind whipped her hair. She could not be quite sure if Michael was in the house already or not, but based on the steadiness of the camera and security systems reporting, there had been no interruptions to service.

Michael was a coward and did not want to face a Sascha who was trained in the art of self-defense and hand-to-hand combat. Sascha suspected Michael would strike while the power was out, either by cutting the power himself or from the force of the storm. And he would try to disorient or disable her in some way.

Entering the house Sascha looked around the massive home. The entire staff had returned to the mainland, and she was completely alone on this island, in this house, with a madman coming for her. She was tired and achy, and although she desperately wanted a hot shower to warm her cold body, she didn't dare make herself vulnerable by being in the shower when Michael could attack her at any moment. Instead she changed into some dry clothes. Clothes she could fight in. Clothes she could run in if she needed to.

After tying her athletic shoes, Sascha left the primary room and made her way down the long corridor back to the main living area. Halfway there the home lost power. Sascha stood in place and held her breath for a moment. She listened for any noise in the home, but all she heard was howling wind and the sound of rain pelting the roof. Pulling her cell phone out of her pocket, she tried to call the island security number, but she had no signal. Putting her phone away, Sascha took a deep breath and continued to slowly walk back to the main area of the home and stopped when she saw a figure across the room.

The only light entering the room was from the full moon. Sascha could barely see anything, but she knew he was there.

"Michael?" Sascha asked, even though she felt certain the figure she saw across the room was Michael Ghant.

Lightning struck the sky, and Sascha was able to see a dripping wet Michael standing across the room from her.

"Finally, we're alone. I have missed you so much, sweetheart," Michael whispered gently as he slowly approached her.

Sascha was slowly moving into an attack stance when Michael said, "I would not do that if I were you," as he held up the gun in his hand.

Sascha did not move out of her stance but kept her eye on Michael's weapon.

"I love you so much, Sascha, and I don't want to hurt you, but tonight you and I are leaving this island together, one way or another."

Out of the corner of Sascha's eye, she saw an illuminated light on the security panel. The backup battery was working, and the system was operational. She needed to hit the panel to alert the police, although in this weather she was not sure anyone would come to her aid and to arrest Michael.

"Michael, put down the gun, and I will go willingly," Sascha said gently.

"See, I so want to believe that, but it's just not in you to give up that easy. And that asshole husband of yours has you so confused you can't see straight. I have been patient. More than patient. I deserve you. We were supposed to be together, you and me. It was always supposed to be me and you in the end," Michael screeched as he became unhinged and sent Sascha's pulse racing.

"Michael, please. I love you, but we cannot be together like this," Sascha pleaded, playing on his emotions. She knew there was only one way off the island, and it was fifty yards away. She had to get to the speedboat at their dock, but first she needed to get past Michael and his gun, and the only way to do that was to keep him talking to buy herself some time.

"Tell me about the first time you realized you loved me," Sascha asked as her eyes darted around the room, looking for the best escape route.

"Don't you remember? You were eight, and I was nine. You were always so fierce and protective of others," Michael said with a look in his eyes that frightened Sascha. "The other boys were always picking on me. They would take my lunch and steal my toy cars and make my life a living hell daily. Then one day you saw what they were doing and stepped in front of me to protect me. You were so beautiful and so brave. I thought for sure they were going to hurt you, but there was something in your eyes that said, 'You do not want to mess with me.' After that I was your shadow. I followed you around like a little puppy dog in love until it turned to true love. I knew you were the one. We were fated to be together, in this life and the next." Michael had a silly smile on his face that made him look maniacal.

He had dropped the gun down to his side, and Sascha saw this as her moment to attack. Running at full force toward Michael, she performed a takedown, sending the gun flying as Sascha knocked Michael to the ground. Wrapping her body around his, Sascha put Michael in a sleeper hold. She pressed her forearm as hard as she could against his throat until he passed out. Feeling his body go limp in her arms, she crawled around in the dark room, hoping to spot the gun. Unable to locate the weapon, and knowing the need to get to safety, Sascha took off out of the house, hitting the emergency button on the panel, and into a full sprint across the property to the docks.

Wind and rain pelted her face and body as she ran in the freezing weather. Making it to the dock, Sascha saw the boat Michael must have used to get there. Removing the line that moored the boat, Sascha used her foot to push the boat away from the dock so Michael would have no way to escape.

She felt relief as she climbed into their speedboat, but that feeling was short-lived as she realized she had no keys to start it. Sascha screamed in frustration before remembering there was a lockbox on the boat that had the extra key, but that box was locked as well. Glancing back up at the dock, she saw the tool and tackle box strapped to the post. Hopping out of the boat, she ran for the box. Pulling the box down, she frantically searched for anything to open the lockbox with. She had found two knives and decided to grab them from the box when she looked up and saw Michael closing in on her with the gun in his hand.

"I didn't want it to be this way, Sascha," Michael said as he raised his arm, keeping some distance between them.

Sascha was prepared to be shot when she heard a horn in the distance and saw the lights of an approaching boat. Michael turned in the direction of the lights, giving Sascha her opportunity to strike. Sascha trusted herself and threw one of the knives in her hand with all her might.

"He's too la—" Michael gurgled as he put his hand to his throat and found the knife in it. Michael fell to the ground and began flailing around in a panic. His hands slipped as he struggled to pull the knife out of his throat, and he began choking to death on his own blood. Sascha walked up and stood over Michael as he lay dying. She kicked the gun away but held the second knife firmly in her hand, while Michael weakly reached out to grab her leg. Michael looked into Sascha's eyes as she watched him take his last breath.

Sascha stood frozen in place, staring at Michael's dead body. She heard her name being called in the distance but continued to stand there in a fog as Devon jumped from the boat and rushed to her.

"Are you okay?" Devon said as he frantically checked his wife for injury.

"Never better," Sascha responded, happy the pouring rain hid her tears of sadness and relief. "How did you get here?" Sascha asked, before noticing Captain Nyles in the distance.

Moments later a police helicopter began circling above their heads.

"Come on, it's going to be a long night. Let's get you into some dry clothes," Devon instructed as he put his arms around Sascha and then led her back to the house.

CHAPTER 34

Sascha sat in her office, at her desk, desperately trying to focus on her writing. It had been months since Michael's death, but he still hung over Sascha's life like a ghost. Though his presence was lessening over time, Sascha was forever changed by the events that transpired on that night on Orcas Island. Her nightmares were back, but as she got further along in her pregnancy, she napped frequently, which helped her get some much-needed rest throughout the day.

Deciding she would not be able to write for now, she turned her attention to the report she had received from a private detective she hired to investigate Marissa Tanner's murder and help Anna in any way that she could. Anna's murder trial was set to start in three months, and Sascha's new baby was due in less than a month. Sascha would have her hands full with her new baby, but she also wanted to be there for her friend. The report had some interesting potential leads, but there was no game-changing information in the report. Sascha would have them keep digging.

As Sascha put away the report, she spotted the two demi

masks in her drawer. Picking them up, she rubbed her fingers across the fabric and then sat the masks on the desk for closer scrutiny. Sascha still had no idea who the masks belonged to and what their connections were to Michael's cave and the Swell. Another mystery to solve, she supposed.

Putting the masks away, Sascha leaned back into her chair. Closing her eyes, she began to relax until she heard large trucks outside. Standing up, Sascha looked out the window to see her new neighbors moving in. She had no idea who had bought Anna's house, but she was interested to meet them. Seeing a luxury vehicle pull up, she put on her sandals and went outside and across the street to introduce herself. She was surprised to find that she had already met her new neighbor. It was Gillian Crafts.

When Gillian saw Sascha walking over, she immediately put down her box and went to hug the very pregnant woman.

"I'm so excited to be your neighbor. I just know we're going to be the best of friends."

Sascha just smiled in response and asked if Gillian needed anything. Gillian declined assistance but said she and her husband, Xavier, would like to have her and Devon over for a visit or dinner as soon as they were settled in.

"We would love that, thank you. Take care and happy unpacking."

Gillian was very nice, Sascha thought as she walked back across the street, but also too eager to be her bestie. Sascha hated that she had become so jaded and closed off to letting new people in her life, but she had been burned one too many times in the past to be so trusting with strangers. The fact that Gillian had been friends with Marissa gave her a strike against her, but she did seem like a genuine person. Sascha decided she would proceed with caution with her new neighbor but be open to getting to know her better.

Walking back to her house, Danielle's swim instructor was just arriving. Little Danielle loved the water and was becoming quite an impressive swimmer. When Sascha and the swim instructor entered the house, Lena was coming down the stairs with Danielle all ready for pool time.

It was a perfect day for relaxing and lounging by the pool. As the group headed out to the backyard pool, Sascha quickly grabbed an extra towel, a bottle of water, a big hat, a romance novel, and her flip-flops. At three years old, Danielle was already a strong, confident swimmer, able to tread water and swim the length of their pool. She was growing up so fast and was so much like her mother Sascha had to smile to herself.

Life was good. Sascha had a new life growing inside of her, a loving, wonderful husband, and her mini-me daughter Danielle who was the light of her life. As she watched Danielle have her swim lessons, she dangled her feet in the pool and soaked up the warm sunrays. Hearing footsteps she turned to see Devon taking a seat on the pool's edge beside her.

"Shouldn't you be working?" Sascha teased as Devon rolled up the bottoms of his slacks, while she looked like the epitome of a vacationer in a sundress, large sunglasses, and a floppy sun hat.

"Not at the moment," he responded as he rubbed her back, which always seemed to ache nowadays. Staring at his lovely wife, Devon asked, "How are you feeling?"

"Good," she tentatively responded, thinking it was a loaded question.

"I ask because I know you. You have to have a million projects and activities all happening at the same time. You thrive on stress and pressure. So I guess my question is, what are you thinking about doing next? A new book series? Starting a charity? I know you have something in mind."

"As a matter of fact, I do."

"And what's that?"

"I think I want to solve Marissa Tanner's murder."

Devon shook his head at her words. "Why did I have the feeling you were going to say that?"

"Because you just get me, Mr. Montague." Sascha chuckled as she leaned in to kiss her husband.

A NOTE TO READERS

Thank you for reading my latest book, *The Most Coveted.* If you enjoyed my book, please leave me a review on Amazon.-com. Stay tuned for more adventures with Sascha and Devon. Thank you!